THE DAYS OF
MOHAMMED

MORE WILDSIDE CLASSICS

THE DAYS OF MOHAMMED

ANNA MAY WILSON

WILDSIDE PRESS

THE DAYS OF MOHAMMED

Published in 2006 by Brownstone Books.

PREFACE.

In "The Days of Mohammed," one aim of the author has been to bring out the fact that it is possible to begin the heaven-life on earth. It is hoped that a few helpful thoughts as to the means of attaining this life may be exemplified in the career of the various characters depicted.

An attempt has been made, by constant reference to the best works on Mohammed and Arabia, to render the historical basis strictly correct. Especial indebtedness is acknowledged to the writings of Irving, Burton, and the Rev. Geo. Bush; also to the travels of Burckhardt, Joseph Pitts, Ludovico Bartema and Giovanni Finati, each of whom undertook a pilgrimage to the cities of Medina and Mecca; also to the excellent synopsis of the life and times of Mohammed as given by Prof. Max Müller in the introduction to Palmer's translation of the Koran.

As the tiny pebble cast into the water sends its circling wavelets to the distant shore, so this little book is cast forth upon the world, in the hope that it may exert some influence in bringing hope and comfort to some weary heart, and that, in helping someone to attain a clearer conception of Divine love and companionship, it may, if in never so insignificant a degree, perhaps help on to that time when all shall

> *"Trust the Hand of Light will lead the people,*
> *Till the thunders pass, the spectres vanish,*
> *And the Light is Victor, and the darkness*
> *Dawns into the Jubilee of the Ages."*

PRECEDING EVENTS—SUMMARY.

Yusuf, a Guebre priest, a man of intensely religious temperament, and one of those whose duty it is to keep alive the sacred fire
of the Persian temple, has long sought for a more heart-satisfying
religion than that afforded to him by the doctrines of his country.
Though a man of kindliest disposition, yet so benighted he is that,
led on by a deep study of the mysteries of Magian and Sabæan
rites, he has been induced to offer, in human sacrifice, Imri, the
little granddaughter of Ama, an aged Persian woman, and daughter of an Arab, Uzza, who, though married to a Persian, lives at
Oman with his wife, and knows nothing of the sacrifice until it is
over.

The death of the child, though beneath his own hand, immediately strikes horror to the heart of the priest. His whole soul
revolts against the inhumanity of the act, which has not brought to
him or Ama the blessing he had hoped for, and he rebels against
the religion which has, though ever so rarely, permitted the exercise of such an atrocious rite. He becomes more than ever dissatisfied with the vagueness of his belief. He cannot find the rest which
he desires; the Zendavesta of Zoroaster can no longer satisfy his
heart's longing; his country-people are sunk in idolatry, and,
instead of worshiping the God of whom the priests have a vague
conception, persist in bowing down before the symbols themselves, discerning naught but the objects—the sun, moon, stars,
fire—light, all in all.

Yusuf, indeed, has a clearer idea of God; but he worships him
from afar off, and looks upon him as a God of wrath and judgment
rather than as the Father of love and mercy. In his new spiritual
agitation he conceives the idea of a closer relation with the Lord of
the universe; his whole soul calls out for a vivid realization of God,
and he casts about for light in his trouble.

From a passing stranger, traveling in Persia—a descendant of
those Sabæan Persians who at an early age obtained a footing in
Arabia, and whose influence was, for a time, so strongly marked
through the whole district known as the Nejd, and even down
into Yemen, Arabia-Felix,—Yusuf has learned of a new and
strange religion held by the people of the great peninsula. His
whole being calls for relief from the doubts which harass him. He
is rich and he decides to proceed at once towards the west and to
search the world, if necessary,—not, as did Sir Galahad and the

knights of King Arthur's Table, in quest of the Holy Grail, but in search of the scarcely less effulgent radiance of the beams of Truth and Love.

CHAPTER I.

YUSUF BEGINS HIS SEARCH FOR TRUTH.

"O when shall all my wanderings end,
And all my steps to Thee-ward tend!"

"Peace, oh peace! that thy light wings might now rest upon me! Truth, that thou mightest shine in upon my soul, making all light where now is darkness! Ye spirits that dwell in yon bright orbs far above me, ye that alone are privileged to bow before the Great Creator of the universe, ye that alone may address yourselves to the Great Omnipotent Spirit with impunity, intercede for me, I beseech you! Bow before that Great Sovereign of all wisdom and light, whom we worship through these vague symbols of fire and brightness; plead with him before whom I dare not come, in my behalf. Beseech of him, if he will condescend to notice his most humble priest, that he may lead him into light effulgent, into all truth, and that he may clear from his soul these vapors of doubt which now press upon him in blackest gloom and rack his soul with torment. If I sin in doubting thus, beseech him to forgive me and to lead me to a conception of him as he is. Ye that are his ministers, from your starry spheres guide me! Whether through darkness, thorns, or stony ways, guide me; I shall not falter if I may see the light at last! Oh, grant me peace!"

Thus prayed Yusuf, the Magian priest. He paused. No sound passed from his lips, but he still stood with upraised arms, gazing into the intense depths of the Persian sky, purple, and flecked with golden stars, the "forget-me-nots of the angels."

His priestly vestments were dazzlingly white, and upon his shoulders were fixed two snowy wings that swept downward to the ground. His black beard descended far over his breast, and from the eyes above shone forth the glow of a soul yearning towards the infinite unknown, whose all is God.

Behind him, near the altar of the rounded tower,—round in the similitude of the orbs of light, the sun, moon, and stars,—danced the sacred fire, whose flames were said to have burned unceasingly for nearly one thousand years. The fiery wreaths leaped upwards toward the same purple sky, as if pointing with long, red fingers, in mockery of the priest's devotion; and the ruddy glare, falling upon him as he stood so still there, enveloped him with a halo of light. It gleamed upon his head, upon his uplifted hands, upon the curves of the wings on his shoulders, silhouetting him against the darkness, and lighting his white habiliments until, all motionless as he was, he seemed like a marble statue dazzlingly radiant in the light of one crimson gleam from a sinking sun.

And so he stood, heeding it not, till the moon rose, soft and full; the mountaintops shone with a rim of silver, the valleys far below the temple looked deeper in the shade, and the fire burned low.

Rapt and more rapt grew the face of the priest. Surely the struggle of his soul was being answered, and in his nearness to Nature, he was getting a faint, far-off gleam of the true nature of Nature's God. His glance fell to the changing landscape below; his arms were extended as if in benediction; and his lips moved in a low and passionate farewell to his native land. Then he turned.

The fire burned low on the altar.

"Sacred symbol, whose beams have no power to warm my chilled heart, I bid you a long farewell! They will say that Yusuf is faithless, a false priest. They will mayhap follow him to slay him. And they will bow again to yon image, and defile thine altars again with infants' blood, not discerning the true God. Yet he must be approachable. I feel it! I know it! O Great Spirit, reveal Thyself unto Yusuf! Reveal Thyself unto Persia! Great Spirit, guide me!"

For the first time, Yusuf thus addressed a prayer direct to the Deity, and he did so in fear and trembling.

A faint gleam shone feebly amid the ashes of the now blackening altar. It flared up for an instant, then fell, and the sacred fire of the Guebre temple was dead.

"The embers die!" cried the priest. "Yea, mockery of the Divine, die in thine ashes!"

He waited no longer, but strode with swift step down the mountain, and into the shade of the valley. Reaching, at last, a cave in the side of a great rock, he entered, and stripped himself of his priestly garments. Then, drawing from a recess the garb of an ordinary traveler, he dressed himself quickly, rolled his white robes into a ball, and plunged farther into the cave. In the darkness the rush of falling water warned him that an abyss was near. Dropping on his knees, he crept carefully forward until his hand rested on the jagged edge of a ledge of rock. Beside him the water fell into a yawning gulf. Darkness darker than blackest night was about him, and, in its cover, he cast the robes into the abyss below, then retraced his way, and plunged once more into the moonlight, a Persian traveler wearing the customary loose trousers, a kufiyah on his head, and bearing a long staff in his hand.

CHAPTER II.

A BEDOUIN ENCAMPMENT.

"The cares that infest the day
Shall fold their tents, like the Arabs,
And as silently steal away."
—Longfellow.

Many months after the departure of Yusuf from Persia a solitary rider on a swift dromedary reached the extreme northern boundary of El Hejaz, the province that stretches over a considerable portion of western Arabia. His face was brown like leather from exposure, and his clothes were worn and travel-stained, yet it scarcely required a second glance to recognize the glittering eyes of the Magian priest.

It seemed as if the excitement of danger and the long days of toil and privation had at last begun to tell upon his iron frame. His eye, accustomed by the fear of robbers to dart its dark glances restlessly, was less keen than usual; his head was drooped downward upon his breast, and his whole attitude betokened bodily fatigue. His camel, too, went less swiftly, and picked its way, with low, plaintive moans, over the rough and precipitous path which led into a wild and weird glen.

It was evening, and the shadows fell in fantastic streaks and blotches across the arid valley, through whose barren soil huge, detached rocks of various-colored sandstone rose in eerie, irregular masses, veritable castles of genii of the uncanny spot.

Yusuf looked uneasily around, but neither sight nor sound of life was near, and he again allowed his faithful beast to slacken its pace and crop a few leaves of the coarse camel-thorn, the only sign of vegetation in the deserted place.

A few trees, however, could be seen in the distance, and he urged his camel towards them in the hope of finding some water, and some dates for food. Reaching the spot, he found that a stagnant pool lay below, but there were no dates on the trees, and the water was brackish. A couple of red-legged partridges fluttered off, cackling loudly as they went. He would fain have had them for food, but their presence seemed like company to the poor wanderer, and he did not attempt to secure them; so, throwing himself at full length on the ground, he flung his arms across his eyes to shield them from the white glare of the sky.

Suddenly a step sounded near. Yusuf started to his feet and grasped his scimitar, but he was instantly beset by half a dozen wild Arabs, who dashed upon him, screaming their wild Arabian jargon, and waving their short swords over their heads.

Blows fell thick and fast. Yusuf had a dazed consciousness of seeing the swarthy, wrinkled visages and gleaming teeth of his opponents darting in confusion before him, of hacking desperately, and of receiving blows on the head; then a sudden gush of blood from a wound on his forehead blinded him, and he fell.

All seemed over. But a shout sounded close at hand. Several Arabs, splendidly mounted on nimble Arabian horses, and waving their long, tufted spears, appeared on the scene. The Bedouin robbers fled precipitately, and Yusuf's first sensation was that of being gently raised, and of feeling water from the pool dashed upon his face.

The priest had not been severely wounded, and soon recovered enough to proceed with the party which had rendered him such timely aid.

An hour's ride brought them to the head of another and more fertile glen or wady, through which a mountain stream wended its way between two bands of tolerably good pasturage. A full moon in all its brilliancy was just rising. Its cold, clear light flooded the wady, bringing out every feature of the landscape with remarkable distinctness. At some distance lay a group of tents, black, and pitched in a circle, as the tents of the Bedouins usually are. Campfires studded the valley with glints of red; and the barking of dogs and shouts of men arose on the night air above the hoarse moanings of the camels. Yusuf was indeed glad to see evidences of Arab civilization, and to look forward to the prospect of a good supper and a friendly bed.

The return of the party was now noticed by the men of the encampment. A group of horsemen, also armed with long spears tufted with ostrich feathers, left the tents and came riding swiftly and gracefully towards their returning companions.

An explanation of Yusuf's sorrowful plight was given, and he was conducted to the tent of the Sheikh, which was marked by being larger than the rest, and situated in the center of the circle, with a spear placed upright in the ground before the door.

The Sheikh himself received the stranger at the door of his tent. He was a middle-aged man, of tall and commanding appearance, though the scowl habitual to the Bedouins by reason of their constant exposure to the sun, rested upon his face. He wore a kufiyah, or kerchief, of red and yellow on his head, the ends falling on his shoulders behind in a crimson fringe. His hair was black and greased, and his eyes, though piercing, were not unkindly. His person was thin and muscular, but he wore gracefully the long abba or outer cloak, white and embroidered, which opened in front, disclosing an undergarment of figured muslin, bound by a crimson sash. And there was native grace in every movement when he came courteously forward and saluted Yusuf with the "Peace be with you" of the Arabs. He then extended his hand to help the traveler to dismount, and led him into the tent.

"Friend," he said, "a long journey and a close acquaintance with death are, methinks, a good preparation for the enjoyment of Bedouin hospitality, which, we sincerely hope, shall not be lacking in the tents of Musa. Yet, in truth, it seems to us that thou art a foolhardy man to tempt the dangers of El Hejaz singlehanded."

"So it has proved," returned the priest; "but a Persian, no more than an Arab, will draw back at the first scent of danger. Yet I deplore these delays, which but hinder me on my way. I had hoped long ere this to be at the end of my journey."

"We will hear all this later," returned the Bedouin with quiet dignity; "for the present, suffice it to keep quiet and let us wash this blood from your hair. Hither, Aswan! Bring warm water, knave, and let the traveler know that the Arab's heart is warm too. Now, friend-stranger, rest upon these cushions, and talk later, if it please you."

With little enough reluctance, Yusuf lay down upon the pile of rugs and cushions, and, while the attendants bathed his brow, looked somewhat curiously about him.

By the light of a dim lamp and a torch or two, he could see that the tent was divided into two parts, as are all Bedouin tents, by a central curtain. This curtain was occasionally twitched aside far enough to reveal a pair of black eyes, and, from the softness of the voices which sounded from time to time behind the folds, he surmised correctly that this apartment belonged to the chief's women.

Several men entered the tent, all swarthy, lithe and sinewy, with the scowling faces and even, white teeth characteristic of the typical Arab. They gesticulated constantly as they talked; but Yusuf, though thoroughly familiar with the Arabic language, paid little attention to the conversation, giving himself up to what seemed to him, after his adventures, perfect rest.

Presently the chief's wife entered. She was unveiled, and her features were distinctly Hebrew; for Lois, wife of the Bedouin Musa, had been born a Jewess. She was dressed in a flowing robe of black confined by a crimson girdle. Strings of coins and of blue opaque beads hung upon her breast and were wound about her ankles, and she wore a black headdress also profusely decorated with beads and bangles of silver.

On a platter she carried some cakes, still smoking hot. These she placed on a low, circular table of copper. A wooden platter of boiled mutton was next added, along with a caldron filled with wheat boiled in camel's milk, and some cups of coffee.

Yusuf was placed at the table, and Musa, after sipping a little coffee, handed the cup to him; the chief then picked out the most savory bits of mutton, and, according to Arabian etiquette, handed them to his guest.

Several men gathered around to partake of the banquet. They crouched or reclined on the ground, about the low table; yet, savage looking though they were, not one of the Bedouins ventured an inquisitive question or bestowed a curious glance on the Persian.

Among them, however, was a little, inquisitive looking man, whose quick, birdlike movements attracted Yusuf's attention early in the evening. His round black eyes darted into every place and upon every one with an insatiable curiosity, and he talked almost incessantly. He was a Jewish peddler who traded small wares with the Arabs, and who was constantly somewhere on the road between Syria and Yemen, being liable to appear suddenly at the most mysterious times, and in the most unlikely places.

In his way, Abraham of Joppa was a character, and one may be pardoned for bestowing more than a passing glance upon him. Though permitted to eat at the table with the rest, it was evident that the Arabs looked upon him with some contempt. They enjoyed listening to his stories, and to his recital of the news which he picked up in his travels, but they despised his inquisitiveness, and resented the impertinence with which he coolly addressed himself even to the Sheikh, before whom all were more or less reserved.

The Persian was, for the present, the chief object of the little Jew's curiosity, and as soon as the meal was over he hastened to form his acquaintance.

Sitting down before the priest, and poising his head on one side, he observed:

"You are bound for the south, stranger?"

"Even so," said Yusuf, gravely.

"Whither?"

"I seek for the city of the great temple."

"Phut! The Caaba!" exclaimed the Jew, with contempt. "Right

well I know it, and a fool's game they make of it, with their running, and bowing, and kissing a bit of stone in the wall as though
'twere the dearest friend on earth!"

"But they worship—"

"A statue of our father Abraham, and one of Ishmael, princi-
pally. A precious set of idolaters they all are, to be sure!"

Yusuf's heart sank. Was it only for this that he had come his
long and weary way, had braved the heat of day and the untold
dangers of night? In searching for that pure essence, the spiritual,
that he craved, had he left the idolatrous leaven at home only to
come to another form of it in Mecca?

"But then," he thought, "this foolish Jew knows not whereof
he speaks: one with the empty brain and the loose tongue of this
wanderer has not probed the depths of divine truth."

"You cannot be going to Mecca as a pilgrim?" hazarded the
little man. "The Magians and the Sabæans worship the stars, do
they not?"

"Alas, yes!" said the priest. "They have fallen away from the
ancient belief. They worship even the stars themselves, and have
set up images to them, no longer perceiving the Great Invisible,
the Infinite, who can be approached only through the mediation
of the spirits who inhabit the starry orbs."

"Methinks you will find little better in Mecca. What are you
going there for?" asked the Jew abruptly.

"I seek Truth," replied the priest quietly.

"Truth!" repeated the Jew. "Aye, aye, the Persian traveler seeks
truth; Abraham, the Jew, seeks myrrh, aloes, sweet perfumes of
Yemen, silks of India, and purple of Tyre. Aye, so it is, and I think
Abraham's commodity is the more obtainable and the more prac-
tical of the two. Yet they do say there are Jews who have sought for
truth likewise; and they tell of apostles who gave up their trade
and fisheries to go on a like quest after a leader whom many Jews
will not accept."

"Who were the apostles?"

"Oh, Jews, of course."

"Where may I find them?"

"All dead, well-nigh six hundred years ago," returned the Jew,
indifferently.

Yusuf's hopes sank again. He longed for even one kindred
spirit to whom he could unfold the thoughts that harassed him.

"I do not know much about what they taught," continued the
Jew. "Never read it; it does not help in my business. But I got a bit
of manuscript the other day from Sergius, an old Nestorian monk

away up in the Syrian hills. I am taking it down to Mecca. I just peeped into it, but did not read it; because it is the people who live now, who have gold and silver for Abraham, that interest him, not those who died centuries ago; and the bit of writing is about such. However, you seem to be interested that way, so I will give it to you to read."

So saying, the Jew unpacked a heavy bundle, and, after searching for some time, upsetting tawdry jewelry, kerchiefs, and boxes of perfume, he at last succeeded in finding the parchment.

He handed it to the Persian. "I hope it may be of use to you, stranger. Abraham the Jew knows little and cares less for religion, but he would be sorry to see you bowing with yon heathen Arab herd at Mecca."

"Dog! Son of a dog!"

It was Musa. Able to restrain his passion no longer, he had sprung to his feet and stood, with flashing eyes and drawn scimitar, in resentment of the slur on his countrymen.

With a howl of fear, the little Jew sprang through the door and disappeared in the darkness.

Musa laughed contemptuously.

"Ha, lack-brained cur!" he said, "I would not have hurt him, having broken bread with him in mine own tent! Yet, friend Persian, one cannot hear one's own people, and one's own temple, the temple of his fathers, desecrated by the tongue of a lackbrained Jew trinket-vender."

"You know, then, of this Caaba—of the God they worship there?" asked the priest.

Musa shook his head, and made a gesture of denial.

"Musa knows little of such things," he replied. "Yet the Caaba is a name sacred in Arabian tradition, and as such, it suits me ill to hear it on the tongue of a craven-hearted Jew. In sooth, the coward knave has left his trumpery bundle all open as it is. I warrant me he will come back for it in good time."

A dark haired lad in a striped silk garment here passed through the tent.

"Hither, Kedar!" called the Sheikh. "Recite for our visitor the story of Moses."

The lad at once began the story, reciting it in a sort of chant, and accompanying his words with many a gesture. The company listened breathlessly, now giving vent to deep groans as the persecution of the children of Israel was described, now bowing their heads in reverence at the revelation of the burning bush, now waving their arms in excitement and starting forward with flashing eyes as the lad pictured the passage of the Red Sea.

Yusuf had heard some vague account of the story before, but, with the passionate nature of the Oriental, he was strangely moved as he listened to the recital of how that great God whom he longed to feel and know had led the children of Israel through all their wanderings and sufferings to the promised land. He felt that he too was indeed a wanderer, seeking the promised land. He was but an infant in the true things of the Spirit. Like many another who longs vainly for a revelation of the working of the Holy Spirit, his soul seemed to reach out hopelessly.

But who can tell how tenderly the same All-wise Creator treasures up every outreaching of the struggling soul! Not one throb of the loving and longing heart is lost;—and Yusuf was yet, after trial, to rejoice in the serene fullness of such light as may fall upon this terrestrial side of death's dividing line.

Poor Yusuf, with all his Persian learning and wisdom, had, through all his life, known only a religion tinctured with idolatry. Almost alone he had broken from that idolatry, and realized the unity of God and his separation from all connected with such worship; but he was yet to understand the connection of God with man, and to taste the fullness of God's love through Christ. He had not realized that the finger of God is upon the life of every man who is willing to yield himself to Divine direction, and that there is thus an inseparable link between the Creator and the creature. He was not able to say, as said Carlyle in these later days, "A divine decree or eternal regulation of the universe there verily is, in regard to every conceivable procedure and affair of man; faithfully following this, said procedure or affair will prosper . . . . Not following this, . . . destruction and wreck are certain for every affair." And what could be better? Divine love, not divine wrath, over all! Yusuf had an idea of divine wrath, but he failed to see—because the presentation of the never-failing Fatherhood of God had not yet come—the infinite love that makes Jesus all in all to us, heaven wherever he is, and hell wherever he is not.

Since leaving Persia, this was the first definite opportunity he had had of listening to Bible truth.

"Kedar knows more of this than his father," explained Musa. "'Tis his mother who teaches him. She was a Jewess, of the people of Jesus of Nazareth, but I fear this roving life has caused my poor Lois to forget much of the teaching of her people."

"You speak of Jesus of Nazareth. I have heard something of him. Tell me more."

Musa shook his head slowly. "I know nothing," he said. "But I shall call Lois. The men have all gone from the tent, and mayhap she can tell what you want."

So saying, he entered the women's apartment, and sent his wife to Yusuf.

"You wish to know of Jesus of Nazareth?" she said. "Alas, I am but a poor teacher. I am unworthy even to speak his name. I married when but a child, and since then I have wandered far from him, for there have been few to teach me. Yet I know that he was in very truth the Son of God. He was all-good. He healed the sick on this earth, and forgave sin. Then, woe, woe to me!—he was crucified,—crucified by my people! And he went up to heaven; his disciples saw him go up in the white clouds of a bright day."

"Where dwells he now? Is he one of the spirits of the stars?"

"I know not. He is in heaven."

"And does he stoop to take notice of us, the children of earth?"

"Alas, I know not! There was once a time when Jesus was more than a name to me. When I knelt, a child, beside my mother on the grassy hills of Hebron, it seemed that Jesus was, in some vague way, a reality to me; but long years of forgetfulness have passed since then. Stranger, I wish you well. Your words have brought back to me the desire to know more of him. If you learn aught of him, and it ever lies in your way to do so, come and tell us,—my Musa and me,—that we too may learn of him."

Rising to her feet, the woman saluted the Persian and left him. Musa entered to conduct him to the rugs set apart for his couch, and soon all was silent about the encampment.

But ere he fell asleep, Yusuf went out into the moonlight. The night was filled with the peculiar lightness of an Oriental night. The moon blazed down like a globe of molten silver, and a few large stars glowed with scarcely secondary brilliance. In the silvery brightness he could easily read the manuscript given him by the Jew. It was the story of the man with the withered hand, whose infirmity was healed by Jesus in the synagogue. And there, in the starlight, the priest bowed his head, and a throng of pentup emotions throbbed in his breast.

"Spirits of the stars, show me God. If this Jesus be indeed the Son of God, show me him. Give me faith, such faith as had he of the withered hand, that I too may stretch forth my hand and be made whole; that I may look, and in looking, see."

This was his prayer. Ah, yet, the "spirits of the stars" were as a bridge to the gulf which, he fancied, lay between him and Infinite Mercy.

CHAPTER III.

YUSUF MEETS AMZI, THE MECCAN.

"Mecca's pilgrims, confident of Fate,
And resolute in heart."
　　　　　　　　　—Longfellow.

The next morning, Yusuf, against the remonstrances of Musa and his wife, prepared to proceed on his way. Like the Ancient Mariner, he felt forced to go on, "to pass like night from land to land," until he obtained that which he sought.

When he was almost ready to depart, a horseman came galloping down the valley, with the news that a caravan, en route for Mecca, was almost in sight, and would make a brief halt near the stream by which Musa's tents were pitched. Yusuf at once determined to avail himself of the timely protection on his journey.

Presently the caravan appeared, a long, irregular line—camels bearing "shugdufs," or covered litters; swift dromedaries, mounted by tawny Arabs whose long Indian shawls were twisted about their heads and fell in fringed ends upon their backs; fiery Arabian horses, ridden by Arabs swaying long spears or lances in their hands; heavily laden packmules, whose leaders walked beside them, urging them on with sticks, and giving vent to shrill cries as they went; and lastly a line of pilgrims, some trudging along wearily, some riding miserable beasts, whose ribs shone through their roughened hides, while others rode, in the proud security of ease and affluence, in comfortable litters, or upon animals whose sleek and well-fed appearance comported with the self satisfied air of their riders.

A halt was called, and immediately all was confusion. Tents were hurriedly thrown up; the packmules were unburdened for a moment; the horses, scenting the water, began to neigh and sniff the air; infants, who had been crammed into saddlebags with their heads out, were hauled from their close quarters; the horsemen of Musa, still balancing their tufted spears, dashed in and out; while his herdsmen, anxious to keep the flocks from mixing with the caravan, shrieked and gesticulated, hurrying the flocks of sheep off in noisy confusion, and urging the herds of dromedaries on with their short, hooked sticks. It was indeed a babel, in which Yusuf had no part; and he once more seized the opportunity of looking at the precious parchment To his astonishment, he perceived that it was addressed to "Mohammed, son of Abdallah, son of Abdal Motalleb, Mecca," with the subscription, "From Sergius the Monk, Bosra."

Here then, Yusuf had, in perfect innocence, been entrapped into reading a communication addressed to some one else, and he smiled sarcastically as he thought of the inquisitiveness of the little Jew who had taken the liberty of "just peeping in."

It remained, now, for Yusuf to find the Jew and to put him again in possession of his charge. He searched for him through the motley crowd, but in vain; then, recollecting that the peddler's bundle had been left behind, he sought Musa, to see if he had heard anything of the little busybody.

Musa laughed heartily. "Remember you not that I said his trumpery would be gone in the morning? I was no false prophet. The man is like a weasel. When all sleep he finds his way in and helps himself to what he will: when all wake, no Jew is to be seen; trumpery and all have gone, no one knows whither."

So the priest found himself responsible for the delivery of the manuscript to this Mohammed, of whom he had never hitherto heard; and, knowing the contents, he was none the less ready to carry out the trust, hoping to find in Mohammed some one who could tell him more of the same wondrous story. He therefore placed the parchment very carefully within the folds of his garment, bade farewell to Musa and his household, and prepared to leave with the caravan, which had halted but a short time on account of the remarkable coolness of the day.

"Peace be with you!" said the Sheikh; "and if you ever need a friend, may it be Musa's lot to stand in good stead to you. I bid you good speed on your journey. We have no fears for your safety now, besides the safety of numbers, the holy month of Ramadhan[1] begins today, and even the wildest of the Bedouin robbers usually refrain from taking life in the holy months. Again, Peace be with you! And remember that the Bedouin can be a friend."

Yusuf embraced the chieftain with gratitude, and took his place in the train, which was already moving slowly down the wady.

As it often happens that in the most numerous concourse of people one feels most lonely, so it was now with Yusuf. There

---

1   The month of Ramadhan was held as holy prior to Mohammed's time; its sanctity was but confirmed by him.

seemed none with whom he cared to speak. Most of the people were self satisfied traders busied with the care of the merchandise which they were taking down to dispose of at the great fair carried on during the Ramadhan. A few were Arabs of the Hejaz, short and well-knit, wearing loose garments of blue, drawn back at the arms enough to show the muscles standing out like whip-cords. Some were smoking short chibouques, with stems of wood and bowls of soft steatite colored a yellowish red. As they rode they used no stirrups, but crossed their legs before and beneath the pommel of the saddle; while, as the sun shone more hotly, they bent their heads and drew their kufiyahs far over their brows. Many poor and somewhat fanatical pilgrims were interspersed among the crowd, and here and there a dervish, with his large, bag-sleeved robe of brown wool—the Zaabut, worn alike by dervish and peasant—held his way undisturbed.

Yusuf soon ceased to pay any attention to his surroundings, and sat, buried in his own thoughts, until a voice, pleasant and like the ripple of a brook, aroused him.

"What thoughts better than the thoughts of a Persian? None. Friend, think you not so?"

The words were spoken in the Persian dialect, and the priest looked up in surprise, to see a ruddy faced man smiling down upon him from the back of a tall, white Syrian camel. He wore the jubbeh, or cloak, the badge of the learned in the Orient; his beard was turning slightly gray, and his eyes were keen and twinkling.

"One question mayhap demands another," returned Yusuf. "How knew you that I am a Persian? I no longer wear Persian garb."

"What! Ask an Arab such a question as that!" said the other, smiling. "Know you not, Persian, that we of the desert lands are accustomed to trace by a mark in the sand, the breaking of a camel-thorn, things as difficult? The stamp of one's country cannot be thrown off with one's clothes. Nay, more; you have been noted as one learned among the Persians."

Yusuf bent his head in assent. "Truly, stranger, your penetration is incomprehensible," he said, with a touch of sarcasm.

"No, no!" returned the other, good humoredly; "but, marking you out for what you are, I thought your company might, perchance, lessen the dreariness of the way. I am Amzi, the Meccan. Some call me Amzi the rich Meccan; others, Amzi the learned; others, Amzi the benevolent. For myself, I pretend nothing, aspire to nothing but to know all that may be known, to live a life of ease, at peace with all men, and to help the needy or unfortunate where

I may. More than one stranger has not been sorry for meeting Amzi the benevolent, in Mecca. Have you friends there?"

"None," said Yusuf. "Yet there is a tradition among our people that the Guebres at one time had temples even in the land of Arabia. Have you heard aught of it?"

"It is said that at one time fire-temples were scattered throughout this land, each being dedicated to the worship of a planet; that at Medina itself was one dedicated to the worship of the moon and containing an image of it. It is also claimed that the fire-worshipers held Mecca, and there worshiped Saturn and the moon, from whence comes their name of the place—Mahgah, or moon's place. The Guebres also hold here that the Black Stone is an emblem of Saturn, left in the Caaba by the Persian Mahabad and his successors long ago. But, friend, Persian influence has long since ceased in El Hejaz. Methinks you will find but few traces of your country-people's glory there."

"It matters not," returned the priest. "The glory of the fire-worshipers has, so far as Yusuf is concerned, passed away. Know you not that before his eyes the sacred fire, kept alive for well-nigh one thousand years, went out in the supreme temple ere he left it? May the great Omniscient Spirit grant that Persia's idolatries will die out in its ashes!"

"And think you that there is no idolatry in Mecca? Friend, believe me, not a house in Arabian Mecca which does not contain its idol! Not a man of influence who will start on an expedition without beseeching his family gods for blessing!"

"And do they not recognize a God over all?"

"They acknowledge Allah as the highest, the universal power,—yet he is virtually but a nominal deity, for they deem that none can enter into special relationship with him save through the mediation of the household gods. In his name the holiest oaths are sworn, nevertheless in true worship he has the last place. Indeed, it must be confessed that neither fear of Allah nor reverence of the gods has much influence over the mass of our people."

"What, then, is the meaning of this great pilgrimage, whose

2   Medina at this time bore the name of Yathrib, but in this volume we shall give it the later and better known name of "Medina," derived from the earlier "Mahdinah."

3   The Moslems *now* assert that the sacred fire went out of itself at the birth of Mohammed.

fame reached me even in Persia? Does not religious enthusiasm lead those poor wretches, hobbling along behind, to take such a journey?"

Amzi nodded his head slowly. "Religious incentives may move the few," he said. "But, friend, can you not see that barter is the leading object of the greater number—of those well-to-do pilgrims who are superintending the carriage of their baggage so complacently there? The holy months, particularly the Ramadhan, afford a period of comparative safety, a long truce that affords a convenient season for traffic. Alas, poor stranger! you will be sad to find that our city, in the time of the holy fast, becomes a place of buying and selling, of vice and robbery—a place where gain is all and God is almost unknown."

"But you, Amzi; what do you believe of such things?"

"In truth, I know not what to think. Believe in idols I cannot; worship in the Caaba I will not; so that my religion is but a belief in Allah, whom I fear to approach, and whose help and influence I know not how to obtain, a confidence in my own morality, and a consciousness of doing good works."

"Strange, strange!" said the priest, "that we have arrived at somewhat the same place by different ways! Amzi, let us be brothers in the quest! Let us rest neither night nor day until we have found the way to the Supreme God! Amzi, I want to feel him, to know him, as I am persuaded he may be known; yet, like you, I fear to approach him. Have you heard of Jesus?"

"A few among a band of coward Jews who live in the Jewish quarter of Mecca, believe in One whom they call Jesus. The majority of them do not accept him as divine; and among those who do, he seems to be little more than a name of some one who lived and died as did Abraham and Ishmael. His teaching, if, indeed, he taught aught, seems to have little effect upon their lives. They live no better than others, and, indeed, they are slurred upon by all true Meccans as cowardly dogs, perjurers and usurers."

Yusuf sighed deeply. It seemed as though he were following a flitting ignis-fatuus, that eluded him just as he came in sight of it.

The rest of the day was passed in comparative silence. The evening halt was called, and it was decided to spend the night in a grassy basin, traversed by the rocky bed of a mountain stream, a "fiumara," down which a feeble brooklet from recent mountain rains trickled. Owing to the security of the month Ramadhan, it was deemed that a night halt would be safe, and the whole caravan encamped on the spot.

As the shades of the rapidly falling Eastern twilight drew on,

Yusuf sat idly near the door of a tent, looking out listlessly, and listening to the chatter of the people about him.

Not far off a Jewish boy, a mere child, of one of the northern tribes, as shown by his fair hair and blue eyes, sang plaintively a song of the singing of birds and the humming of bees, of the flowers of the North, of rippling streams, of the miraged desert, of the waving of the tamarisk and the scent of roses.

Yusuf observed the childlike form and the effeminate paleness of the cherub face, and a feeling of protective pity throbbed in his bosom as he noted the slender smallness of the hand that glided over the one-stringed guitar, showing by its movements, even in the fading evening light, the blue veins that coursed beneath the transparent skin. He called the lad to his side, and bade him sing to him. Not till then did he notice the vacancy of the look which bespoke a slightly wandering mind. Yusuf's great heart filled with sympathy.

"Poor lad!" he said, "singing all alone! Where are your friends?"

"Dumah's friends?" said the child, wonderingly. "Poor Dumah has no friends now! He goes here and there, and people are kind to him—because Dumah sings, you know, and only angels sing. He tells them of flocks beside the pool, of lilies of Siloam, of birds in the air and angels in the heavens—then everyone is kind. Ah! the world is fair!" he continued, with a happy smile. "The breeze blows hot here, sometimes, but so cool over the sea; and the lilies blow in the vales of Galilee, and the waves ripple bright over the sea where he once walked."

"Who, child?"

"Jesus—don't you know?" with a wondering look. "He sat often by the Lake of Galilee where I have sat, and the night winds lifted his hair as they do mine, and he smiled and healed poor suffering and sinful people. Ah, he did indeed! Poor Dumah is talking sense now, good stranger; sometimes he does not—the thoughts come and go before he can catch them, and then people say, 'Poor little Dumah is demented.' But if Jesus were here now, Dumah would be healed. I dreamed one night I saw him, and he smiled, and looked upon me so sweetly and said, 'Dumah loves me! Dumah loves me!' and then I saw him no more. Friend, I know you love him, too. What is your name?"

"Yusuf."

"Then, Yusuf, you will be my friend?"

"I will be your friend, poor Dumah!"

"Oh, no, Dumah is not poor! He is happy. But his thoughts are going now. Ah, they throng! The visions come! The birds and the mists and the flowers are twining in a wreath, a wreath that stretches up to the clouds! Do you not see it?" and he started off again on his wild, plaintive song.

Yusuf's eyes filled with tears, and he drew the lad to his bosom, and looked out upon the grassy plot before the door, where a huge fire was now shedding a flickering and fantastic glare upon the wrinkled visages of the Arabs, and lighting up the scene with a weird effect only to be seen in the Orient.

Caldrons were boiling, and a savory odor penetrated the air. Men were talking in groups, and a little dervish was spinning around nimbly in a sort of dance. Yusuf looked at him for a moment. There seemed to be something familiar about his figure and movements, but in the darkness he could not be distinctly seen, and Yusuf soon forgot to pay any attention to him.

He drew the boy, who had now fallen asleep, close to him. What would he, Yusuf, not give to learn fully of that source from whence the few meagre crumbs picked up by this poor child were yet precious enough to give him, all wandering as he was at times, the assurance of a sympathetic God, and render him happy in the realization of his presence! What must be the joy of a full revelation of these blessed truths, if, indeed, truths they were!

The longing for such companionship filled Yusuf, as he lay there, with an intense desire. He could scarcely define, in truth he scarcely understood, exactly what he wanted. There was a lack in his life which no human agency had, as yet, been able to satisfy. His heart was "reaching out its arms" to know God—that was all; and he called it searching for Truth.

Far into the night the Persian pondered, his mind beating against the darkness of what was to him the great mystery; and he prayed for light. He thought of the Father, yet again he prayed to the spirits of the planets which were shining so brightly above him. But did not an echo of that prayer ascend to the throne of grace? Was not the eye of Him who notes even the sparrows when they fall, upon his poor, struggling child?

And the end was not yet.

CHAPTER IV.

WHEREIN YUSUF ENCOUNTERS A SANDSTORM IN THE DESERT, AND HAS SOMEWHAT OF AN EXPERIENCE WITH THE LITTLE DERVISH.

"A column high and vast,
A form of fear and dread."
　　　　　　　—Longfellow.

With but few events worthy of notice the journey to Mecca was concluded. After a short halt at Medina, the caravan set out by one of the three roads which then led from Medina to Mecca.

The way led through a country whose aspect had every indication of volcanic agency in the remote ages of the earth's history. Bleak plains—through whose barren soil outcrops of blackened scoriæ, or sharp edges of black and brittle hornblende, appeared at every turn—were interspersed with wadies, bounded by ridges of basalt and green stone, rising from one hundred to two hundred feet high, and covered with a scanty vegetation of thorny acacias and clumps of camel-grass. Here and there a rolling hill was cut by a deep gorge, showing where, after rain, a mighty torrent must foam its way; and, more rarely still, a stagnant pool of saltish or brackish water was marked out by a cluster of daum palms.

On all sides jackals howled dismally during the night; and above, during the day, an occasional vulture wheeled, fresh from the carcass of some poor mule dead by the wayside.

Such was the appearance of the land through which the caravan wound its way, beneath a sky peculiar to Arabia—purple at night, white and terrible in its heat at noon, yet ever strange, weird and impressive.

But one incident worth recounting occurred on the way. Yusuf, Amzi, and the boy Dumah had been traveling side by side for some time. The way, at that particular spot, led over a plain which afforded comparatively easy traveling, and thus gave a better opportunity for conversation. The talk had turned upon

---

4　A fourth, the "Darb-el-Sharki," or Eastern Road, has since been built by order of the wife of the famous Haroun al Raschid.

the Guebre worship, and the priest was amazed at the knowledge shown by Amzi of a religion so little known in Arabia.

"I can tell you more than that," said Amzi in a low tone. "I can tell you that you are not only Yusuf the Persian gentleman of leisure, but Yusuf the Magian priest, accustomed to feed the sacred fire in the Temple of Jupiter. Is it not so? Did not Yusuf's hand even take the blood of Imri the infant daughter of Uzza in sacrifice? Can Yusuf the Persian traveler deny that?"

Yusuf's head sank; his face crimsoned with pain, and the veins swelled like cords on his brow.

"Alas, Amzi, it is but too true!" he said. "Yet, upon the most sacred oath that a Persian can swear, I did it thinking that the blessing of the gods would thus be invoked. The rite is one not unknown among the Sabæans of today, and common even among the Magians of the past. Amzi, it was in my days of heathendom that I did it, thinking it a duty to Heaven. It was Yusuf the priest who did it, not Yusuf the man; yet Yusuf the man bears the torture of it in his bosom, and seeks forgiveness for the blackest spot in his life! How knew you this, Amzi?—if the question be an honorable one."

"Amzi knows much," returned the Meccan. "He knows, too, that Yusuf can never escape the brand of the priesthood. See!"

He leaned forward, and drew back the loose garment from the Persian's breast. A red burn, or scar, in the form of a torch, appeared in the flesh. As Yusuf hastened to cover it, a head was thrust forward, and two beadlike eyes peered from a shrouded face. It was the little dervish.

The priest was annoyed at the intrusion. He determined to take note of the meddler, but the occurrence of an event common in the desert drove all thought of the dervish from his mind.

The cry "A simoom! A simoom!" arose throughout the caravan.

There, far towards the horizon, was a dense mass of dull, copper colored cloud, rising and surging like the waves of a mad ocean. It spread rapidly upwards toward the zenith, and a dull roar sounded from afar off, broken by a peculiar shrieking whistle. And now dense columns could be seen, bent backward in trailing wreaths of copper at the top, changing and swaying before the hurricane, yet ever holding the form of vapory, yellow pillars,—huge shafts extending from earth to heaven, and rapidly advancing with awful menace upon the terrified multitude.

The Arabs screamed, helpless before the manifestation of what they believed was a supernatural force, for they look upon these columns as the evil genii of the plains. Men and camels fell to the ground. Horses neighed in fear, and galloped madly to and fro. But the hot breath of the "poison wind" was upon them in a moment, shrieking like a fiend among the crisping acacias. The sandstorm then fell in all its fury, half smothering the poor wretches, who strove to cover their heads with their garments to keep out the burning, blistering, pitiless dust.

Fortunately all was over in a moment, and the tempest went swirling on its way northward, leaving a clear sky and a dust-buried country in its wake.

In the confusion the dervish had escaped to the other end of the caravan, and was forgotten.

At the end of the tenth day after leaving Medina the caravan reached the head of the long, narrow defile in which lies the city of Mecca, the chief town of El Hejaz. It was early morning when the procession passed through the cleft at the western end; and the sun was just rising, a globe of red, above the blue mountains towards Tayf, when Yusuf stopped his camel on an eminence in full view of the city. There it lay in the heart of the rough blackish hills, whose long shadows still fell upon the low stone houses and crooked streets beneath.·

The priest's eager glance sought for the Caaba. There it was, a huge, stone cube, standing in the midst of a courtyard two hundred and fifty paces long by two hundred paces wide, and shrouded from top to bottom by a heavy curtain of dark, striped cloth of Yemen.

There was something awe-inspiring in the scene, and the priest felt a thrill of apprehensive emotion as he gazed upon what he had fondly hoped would prove the end of his long journey. Yet his eye clouded; he covered his face with his mantle and wept, saying to his soul, "Here, too, have they turned aside to worship the false, and have bowed down to idols! My soul! My soul! Where shalt thou find truth and rest?"

Amzi touched him on the arm. "Why do you weep, friend? Thou art a false Guebre, truly! Know you not that even they hold the Caaba in high reverence?"

5   Joseph Pitts, A.D. 1680, says: "Mecca is surrounded for several miles with many thousands of little hills which are very near to one another. They are all stony rock, and blackish, and pretty near of a bigness, appearing at a distance like cocks of hay, but all pointing towards Mecca."

There was a tone of good natured raillery in the voice, and the speaker continued: "Arouse yourself, my friend. See how they worship in Mecca. They are at it already! See them run! By my faith 'tis a lusty morning exercise!"

Yusuf looked up to see a great concourse of people gathering in the courtyard. Many were rushing about the Caaba, and pausing frequently at one corner of the huge structure.

"Each pilgrim," explained Amzi, "holds himself bound to go seven times about the temple, and the harder he runs the more virtue there is in it—performing the Tawaf, they call it. Those who seem to pause are kissing the Hajar Aswad—the Black Stone, which, the Arabs say, was once an angel cast from heaven in the form of a pure white jacinth. It is now blackened by the kisses of sinners, but will, at the last day, arise in its angel form, to bear testimony of the faithful who have kissed it, and have done the Tawaf faithfully. And now, friend, come to the house of Amzi, and see if he can be as hospitable as Musa the Bedouin."

Yusuf gratefully accepted the invitation, and the camels were urged on again down the narrow, crooked street.

"Know you aught of one Mohammed?" asked the priest. "A roguish Hebrew left me, with scant ceremony, in possession of a manuscript which must be given to him."

"Aye, well do I know him," said Amzi. "Mohammed, the son of Abdallah the handsome, and grandson of Abdal Motalleb, who was the son of Haschem of the tribe of the Koreish—a tribe which has long held a position among the highest of Mecca, and has, for ages past, had the guardianship of the Caaba itself. Mohammed himself is a man of sagacity and honor in all his dealings. He is married to Cadijah, a wealthy widow, whose business he has long carried on with scrupulous fairness. He, too, is one of the few who, in Mecca, have ceased to believe in idols, and would fain see the Caaba purged of its images."

"There are some, then, who cast aside such beliefs?"

"Yes, the Hanifs (ascetics), who utterly reject polytheism. Waraka, a cousin of the wife of Mohammed, is one of the chief of these; and Mohammed himself has, for several years, been accustomed to retire to the cave of Hira for meditation and prayer. It is said that he has preached and taught for some time in the city, but only to his immediate friends and relatives. Well, here we are at last,"—as a pretentious stone building was reached. "Amzi the benevolent bids Yusuf the Persian priest welcome."

Amzi led the priest into a house furnished with no small degree of Oriental splendor.

"Right to the carven cedarn doors,
Flung inward over spangled floors,
Broad-based flights of marble stairs
Ran up with golden balustrade,
After the fashion of the time."

A meal of Oriental dishes, dried fruit and sweetmeats was prepared; and, when the coolness of evening had come, the two friends proceeded to the temple.

Entering by a western gate, they found the great quadrangle crowded with men, women and children, some standing in groups, with sanctimonious air, at prayers, while others walked or ran about the Caaba, which loomed huge and somber beneath the solemn light of the stars. A few solitary torches—for at that time the slender pillars with their myriads of lamps had not been erected—lit up the scene with a weird, wavering glare, and threw deep shadows across the white, sanded ground.

A curious crowd it seemed. The wild enthusiasm that marked the conduct of the followers of Mohammed at a later day was absent, yet every motion of the motley crowd proclaimed the veneration with which the place inspired the impressionable and excitable Arabs.

Here stood a wealthy Meccan, with flowing robes, arms crossed and eyes turned upward; there stalked a tall and gaunt figure whose black robes and heavy black headdress proclaimed the wearer a Bedouin woman. Here ran a group of beggars; and there a number of half naked pilgrims clung to the curtained walls. Once a corpse was carried into the enclosure and borne in solemn Tawaf round the edifice.

"Look!" cried poor Dumah. "The son of the widow of Nain! The son of the widow of Nain! Oh, why does not he whom Dumah sees in his dreams come to raise him! But then, there are idols here, and he cannot come where there are other gods before him."

On surveying the temple, Yusuf discovered that the door of the edifice was placed seven feet above the ground. Amzi informed him that the temple might be entered only at certain times, but that it contained an image of Abraham holding in its hand some arrows without heads; also a similar statue of Ishmael likewise with divining arrows, and lesser images of prophets and angels amounting almost to the number of three hundred.

Passing round the temple to the north-eastern corner, Yusuf looked curiously at the Black Stone, which was set in the wall at a few spans from the ground, and which seemed to be black with yellowish specks in it. Many people were pressing forward to kiss it, while many more were drinking and laving themselves with water from a well a few paces distant,—the well Zem-Zem,—believing that in so doing their sins were washed off in the water.

"This," said Amzi, pointing to the spring, "is said to be the well which gushed up to give drink to our forefather Ishmael and Hagar his mother, when they had gone into the wilderness to die."

Yusuf sighed heavily. Such empty ceremony had no longer any attraction for him, and he turned his eyes towards the mountain Abu Kubays, towering dark and gloomy above the town, its black crest touched with a silvery radiance by the light of the stars shining brilliantly above.

Was this, then, the Caaba? Was this what he had fondly hoped would fill his heart's longing? Was there any food in this empty ceremonial for a hungering soul? Why, oh why did the truth ever elude him, flitting like an ignis-fatuus with phantom light through a dark and blackened wilderness!

Amzi was talking to someone in the crowd, and Yusuf passed slowly out and11 bent his way down a silent and deserted street. No one was in sight except a very young girl, almost a child, who was gliding quickly on in the shadows. Once or twice she seemed to stagger, then she fell. Yusuf hurried to her, and turned her face to the starlight. Even in that dim light he could see that it was contorted with pain. Yusuf heard the murmur of voices in a low building close at hand, and, without waiting to knock, he lifted the girl in his arms, opened the door, and passed in.

6   Burton says the black stone is volcanic, but is thought by some to be a meteorite or aërolite. Burckhardt thought it composed of lava. Of its appearance Ali Bey says: "It is a block of volcanic basalt, whose circumference is sprinkled with little crystals, with rhombs of tile-red feldspath on a dark background like velvet or charcoal."

CHAPTER V.

NATHAN THE JEW.

"I shall be content, whatever happens, for what God chooses must be better than what I can choose."
—Epictetus.

The same evening on which Yusuf visited the temple, a woman and her two children sat in a dingy little room with an earthen floor, in one of the most dilapidated streets of Mecca. The woman's face bore traces of want and suffering, yet there was a calm dignity and hopefulness in her countenance, and her voice was not despairing. She sat upon a bundle of rushes placed on the floor. No lamp lighted the apartment, but through an opening in the wall the soft starlight shone upon the bands of hair that fell in little braids over her forehead. Her two beautiful children were beside her, the girl with her arm about her mother, and the boy's head on her lap.

"Will we have only hard cake for breakfast, mother, and tomorrow my birthday, too?" he was saying.

"That is all, my little Manasseh, unless the good Father sees fit to send us some way of earning more. You know even the hairs of our heads are numbered, so he takes notice of the poorest and weakest of his children, and has promised us that there will be no lack to them that fear him."

"But, mother, we have had lack many, many times," said the boy thoughtfully.

The mother smiled. "But things have usually come right in the end," she said, "and you know 'Our light affliction, which is but for a moment, worketh for us a far more exceeding and eternal weight of glory.' We cannot understand all these things now, but it will be plain some day. 'We will trust, and not be afraid,' because our trust is in the Lord; and we know that 'he will perfect that which concerneth us,' if we trust him."

"And will he send father home soon?" asked the boy. "We have been praying for him to come, so, so long! Do you think God hears us, mother? Why doesn't he send father home?"

The woman's head drooped, and a tear rolled down her cheek, but her voice was calm and firm.

"Manasseh, child," she said, "your father may never return; but, though a Jew, he was a Christian; and, living or dead, I know he is safe in the keeping of our blessed Lord. Yes, Manasseh, God hears the slightest whisper breathed from the heart of those who call upon him in truth. He says, Jesus says, 'I know my sheep, and am known of mine.' Little son, I like to think that our blessed Savior, who 'laid down his life for the sheep,' is here—in this very room, close to us. Sometimes I close my eyes and think I see him, looking upon us in mercy and love from his tender eyes, and he almost seems so near that I may touch him. No, he will never forsake us. Little ones, my constant prayer for you is that you may learn to realize the depths of his love, and to render him your hearts in return; that you may feel ever closer to him than to any earthly parent, and prove yourselves loving, faithful children of whom he may not be ashamed."

The woman's voice trembled with emotion as she concluded, and a glow of happiness illuminated her thin features.

"Well, mother, I was ashamed today," said little Manasseh. "I got angry and struck a boy."

"Manasseh! My child!"

"You cannot understand, mother; you are so good that you never get angry or wicked. But the anger keeps rising up in me till it seems as if my heart would burst; the blood rushes to my face, my eyes flash—then—I strike, and think of nothing."

She stroked his hair gently. "Manasseh, my boy's temper is one enemy which he has to conquer. But he must not try to conquer it in his own strength. We have an Almighty Helper who has given us to know that he will not suffer us to be tempted beyond that we are able, and has bidden us cast all our care upon him. He will be only too willing to guide us and uphold us by his power, if we will but let him keep us and lead us far from all temptation."

"Then what would you do, mother, if you were in my place when the anger comes up?"

She stooped and kissed him. "I would say, 'Jesus, help me,' and leave it all to him."

Just then a step sounded at the door. Some one entered, and a cry of "Father! Oh, father!" burst from the children. The mother sprang, trembling, to her feet. It was the long-lost husband and father!

Then the lamp was lighted, and the traveler told his loved ones the story of his long absence; how he had embarked at Jeddah on a foist bound for the head of the Red Sea; how he had been shipwrecked; had become ill of a fever as the result of exposure; and how he had at last made his painful way home by traveling overland.

As they thus sat, talking in ecstasy of joy at their reunion, the door opened and Yusuf entered with the girl in his arms.

Water was sprinkled upon her face and she soon recovered. She placed her hand on her brow in a dazed way, then sprang up, and, just pausing for an instant in which her wondrous beauty might be noted, dashed off into the night.

"It is Zeinab, the beautiful child of Hassan," said the Jewess. "She will be well again now. The paroxysms have come before."

"Sit you down, friend," said her husband to Yusuf. "We were just about to break bread. 'Tis a scanty meal," he added, with a smile. "But we have been enjoined to 'be not forgetful to entertain strangers,' because many have thus entertained angels unawares. We shall be glad of the company."

There was a manly uprightness in the look and tone of Nathan the Jew which caught Yusuf's fancy at once, and he sat down without hesitation at the humble board.

And there, in that little, dingy room, he saw the first gleam of that radiant light which was to transform the whole of his after life. He heard of the trials and disappointments, of the heroic fortitude born of that trust in and union with God which he had so craved. He received his first glimpse of a God, human as we are human, who understands every longing, every doubt, every agony that can bleed the heart of a poor child of earth.

He scarcely dared yet to believe that this God was one really with him at all times and in all places, seeing, hearing, knowing, sympathizing. He scarcely dared to realize the possibility of a companionship with him, or the fact that the mediation of the planet-spirits was but a myth. Yet he did feel, in a vague way, that the light was breaking, and a tumultuous, undefined, hopeful ecstasy took possession of his being. Yusuf's heart was ready for the reception of the truth. He was unprejudiced. He had cast aside all dependence upon the tenets of his former belief. He had become as a little child anxious for rest upon its father's bosom. He sought only God, and to him the light came quickly.

There was an infinity of blessed truth to learn yet, but, as he went out into the night, he knew that a something had come into his life, transforming and ennobling it. The divinity within him throbbed heart to heart with the Divinity that is above all, in all, throughout all good. Though vaguely, he felt God; he knew that now, at last, he had entered upon the right road.

Then he thought of Amzi. He must try to tell him all this. Surely Amzi the learned, the benevolent, would rejoice too in hearing the story of Jesus' life on earth, of his coming as an expression of the love of God to man, that man might know God.

Through the dark streets he hastened, thinking, wondering, rejoicing. He sought the bedside of Amzi on the flat roof.

"Amzi, awake!" he cried.

"What now, night-hawk?" said the Meccan, in his good natured, half railing tone. "Why pounce upon a man thus in the midst of his slumbers?"

"Amzi, I have heard glorious news of him—that Jesus of whom we have talked!"

"Well?"

"He seems indeed to be the God for whom I have longed. They have been telling me of his life, yet I realize little save that he came to earth that men might know him; that he died to show men the depth of his love; and that he is with us at every time, in every place—even here, now, on this roof! Only think of it, Amzi! He is close beside us, seeing us, hearing us, knowing our very hearts! There is no need more of appealing to the spirits of the stars. Ah, they were ever far, far off!"

"And where learned you all this, friend priest?" There was an indifferent raillery in the tone which chilled Yusuf to the heart.

"From Nathan, a Christian Jew, and his wife—people who live close to God if any one does."

"In the Jewish quarter?"

"Even so."

Amzi laughed. "Truly, friend, you have chosen a fair spot for your revelation—a quarter of filth and vice. A case of good coming out of evil, truly!"

"Will you not grant that there are some good even in the Jewish quarter?"

"Some, perhaps; yet there are some good among all peoples."

"Amzi, can you not believe?"

"No, no, friend Yusuf; I am glad for your happiness—believe what you will. But it is foreign to Amzi's nature to accept on hearsay that which he has not inquired into—probed to the bottom even. He cannot accept the testimony of any passing stranger, however plausible it may seem. Rejoice if you will, Yusuf, in the spring of a night-tune, but leave Amzi to seek for the deep waters still."

Amzi was now talking quickly and impressively.

Yusuf was amazed. The light was beginning to shine so brightly in his own soul that he could not comprehend why others could not see and believe likewise. He talked with his friend until the dawn began to tint the top of Abu Kubays, but without effect.

At every turn he was met by the bitter prejudice held by the Meccans against the whole Jewish race, a prejudice which kept even Amzi the benevolent from believing in anything advocated by them.

"Why do they not show Christ in their lives, then?" he would say.

"You cannot judge the whole Christian band by the misdeeds of a few, who are, indeed, no Christians," Yusuf pleaded.

"True; yet a religion such as you describe should appeal to more of them, and would, if it were all you imagine it to be. A perfect religion should be exemplified in the lives of those who profess it."

"I grant you that that is true," was Yusuf's reply. "And as an example let me bring you to Nathan and his family. Nobody could talk for one hour to them without feeling that they have found, at least, something which we do not possess. This something, they say, is their God."

"Well, well. I shall do so to please you," said Amzi indifferently, "but I hope that a longer acquaintance may not spoil your trust in these people."

Further expostulation was vain. Yusuf retired to his own apartment, and prayed long and fervently, in his own simple way, offering thanks for the light which was breaking so radiantly on his own soul, and beseeching the loving Jesus to touch the heart of Amzi, who, he knew, though less enthusiastic than he, also desired to know truth.

And before he lay down for a short rest, he said:

"Grant, O Jesus, thou who art ever present, that I may know thee better, and that Amzi, too, may learn to know thee. Reveal thyself to him as thou art revealing thyself to me, that we may know thee as we should."

The priest's face grew radiant with happiness as he concluded.

And yet, in that same city, vice held sway; for, even as the priest prayed, a dark figure emerged from an unused upper attic in the house of Nathan the Jew, and, escaping by a window, descended a garden stair and disappeared in the darkness. Even in that dim light, had one looked he might have noted that the mysterious prowler wore the dress of a dervish.

CHAPTER VI.

YUSUF'S FIRST MEETING WITH MOHAMMED.

> *"A person with abnormal auditory sensations often comes to interpret them as voices of demons, or as the voice of one commanding him to do some deed. This hallucination, in turn, becomes an apperceiving organ, i.e., other perceptions and ideas are assimilated to it: it becomes a center about which many ideas gather and are correspondingly distorted."*
> —McLellan, *Psychology.*

Upon the evening of the following day, Amzi and Yusuf set out in quest of Mohammed, to whom the manuscript had not yet been given. Stopping at the house of Cadijah, a stone building having some pretensions to grandeur, they learned that Mohammed had left the city. Accordingly, thinking he would probably be found in the Cave of Hira, they took a bypath towards the mountains.

The sun was hot, but a pleasant breeze blew from the plains towards the Nejd, and, from the elevation which they now ascended, Yusuf noted with interest a scene every point of which was entirely different from that of his Persian home—different perhaps from that of any other spot on the face of the earth; a scene desolate, wild, and barren, yet destined to be the cradle of a mighty movement that was ere long to agitate the entire peninsula of Arabia, and eventually to exercise its baneful influence over a great part of the Eastern Hemisphere.

Below him lay the long, narrow, sandy valley. No friendly group of palms arose to break its dreary monotony; no green thing, save a few parched aloes, was there to form a pleasant resting place for the eye. The passes below, those ever populous roads leading to the Nejd, Syria, Jeddah, and Arabia-Felix, were crowded with people; yet, even their presence did not suffice to remove the air of deadness from the scene. Of one thing only could the beholder be really conscious—desolation, desolation; a

---

7   By the latest statistics the number of Mohammedans now scattered throughout Asia, Africa, and the south-eastern part of Europe amounts to some 176,834,372.

desolate city surrounded by huge, bare, skeletonlike mountains, grim old Abu Kubays with the city stretching half way up its gloomy side, on the east; the Red mountain on the west; Jebel Kara toward Tayf, and Jebel Thaur with Jebel Jiyad the Greater, on the south.

Yusuf watched the people, many of whom were pilgrims, swarming like so many ants below him towards the Caaba, which was in full view, standing like a huge sarcophagus in the center of the great courtyard. In the transparent air of the Orient, even the pillars supporting the covered portico about the courtyard were quite visible. Yusuf had observed the great system of barter, the buying and selling that went on beneath the roof of that long portico, within the very precincts of the temple set apart for the worship of the Deity, and, as he watched the pigmy creatures, now swarming towards the trading stalls, now hastening to perform Tawaf about the temple, he almost wept that such sacrilege should exist, and a great throb of pity for these erring people whose spiritual nature was barren as the vast, treeless, verdureless waste about them, filled his breast.

Amzi directed his attention towards the east, where the blue mountains of Tayf stood like outposts in the distance.

"There," said he, "at but a three days' journey is the district of plenty, the Canaan of Mecca, whence come the grapes, melons, cucumbers, and pomegranates that are to be seen in our markets. There are pleasant dales and gardens where the camel-thorn gives way to a carpet of verdure; where the mimosa and acacia give place to the glossy-leaved fig tree, to stately palms, and pomegranates of the scarlet fruit; where rippling streams are heard, and the songs of birds fill the air. There is a tradition that Adam, when driven out of the Garden of Eden, settled at Mecca; and there, on the site of the temple yonder, and immediately beneath a glittering temple of pearly cloud, shimmering dews, and rainbow lights said to be in Paradise above,—the Baît-el Maamur of Heaven,—was built, by the help of angels, the first Caaba, a resplendent temple with pillars of jasper and roof of ruby. Adam then compassed the temple seven times, as the angels did the Baît above in perpetual Tawaf. He then prayed for a bit of fertile land, and immediately a mountain from Syria appeared, performed Tawaf round the Caaba, and then settled down yonder at Tayf. Hence, Tayf is even yet called 'Kita min el Sham'—a piece of Syria, the fatherland."

"So then, this Caaba, according to tradition, is of early origin?"

"The Arabs believe that when the earthly Baît-el Maamur was

taken to heaven at Adam's death, a third one was built of stone and mud by Seth. This was swept away by the Deluge, but the Black Stone was kept safe in Abu Kubays, which is, therefore, called 'El Amin'—the Honest. After the flood, a fourth House was built by our father Abraham, to whom the angel Gabriel restored the stone. Abraham's building was repaired and in part restored by the Amalikah tribe. A sixth Caaba was built by the children of Kahtan, into whose tribe, say the Arabs, Ismail was married. The seventh house was built by Kusay bin Kilab, a forefather of Mohammed, and I have reason to believe that he was the first who filled it with the idols which now disgrace its walls. Kusay's house was burnt, its cloth covering (or kiswah) catching fire from a torch. It was rebuilt by the Koreish (Qurâis) a few years ago. It was then that the door was placed high above the ground, as you see it, and then that the movable stair was constructed. Then, too, the six columns which support the roof were added, and Mohammed, El Amin, was chosen to determine the position of the Black Stone in the wall. So, friend, I have now given you in part, the history of the Caaba."

Bestowing a last look upon the temple, the friends walked for some distance northward across the slopes of Mount Hira, until a low, dark opening appeared in the face of a rock.

Drawing back a thorny bush from its door, they entered the cave. A low moaning noise sounded within. For a moment, the transition from the white glare without to the twilight of the cave blinded them, then they saw that the moans proceeded from Mohammed, who was lying on his back on the stone floor. His headdress was awry, his face was purple, and froth issued from his mouth.

Amzi seized an earthen vessel of water, and bathed his brow.

"Poor fellow!" he said, "how often he may have suffered here alone! It has been his custom for years to spend the holy month of Ramadhan here in prayer and meditation. He has often taken these fits before; but, if what is said be true, he knows not that he is suffering, for angels appear to him during the paroxysms."

"It seems to me much more like a fit of epilepsy," said Yusuf, rather sarcastically. "See, he begins to come to himself again."

Mohammed had stopped moaning, and his face began to regain its natural color.

Presently he opened his eyes in a dazed way, and sat up. He was a man of middle height, with a ruddy, rather florid complexion, a high forehead, and very even, white teeth. There was something commanding and dignified in his appearance. He wore a bushy beard, and was habited in a striped cotton gown of cloth of Yemen; and, from his person emanated the sweet odor of choicest perfumes of the Nejd and Arabia-Felix.

"Ah, it is Amzi!" he said. "Pardon me, friend, but the angel has just left me, and I failed to recognize you at once, my mind was so occupied with the wonder of his communications; for, friend, the time is nigh, even at hand, when the prophet of Allah, the One, the only Person of the Godhead, is to be proclaimed!"

His voice was low and musical, and he spoke as one under the influence of an inspiration.

"Has the angel appeared to you in visible form?"

"Sometimes he appears in human form, but in a blinding light; at other times I hear a sound as of a silver bell tinkling afar. Then I hear no words, but the truth sinks upon my soul, and burns itself into my brain, and I feel that the angel speaks."

"Of what, then, has he spoken?" asked Amzi.

"The time in which the full revelation shall be thrown open to man is not yet. But it will come ere long. None, heretofore, save my own kin and friends, have been given aught of the great message; yet to you, Amzi, may I say that Abraham, Moses, Christ, have all been servants of the true God, yet for Mohammed has been reserved the honor of casting out the idolatry with which the worship of our people reeks. For him is destined the glory of purging our Caaba of its images, and of reinstating the true religion of our fathers in this fair land. Then shall men know that Allah is the one God, and Mohammed is his prophet!"

"Think you to place yourself on an equality with the Son of God?" cried Yusuf, sternly.

Mohammed turned quickly upon him, and his face worked in a frenzy of excitement.

"I tell you there is but one God,—one invisible, eternal God, Allah above all in earth and heaven,—and Mohammed is the prophet of God!" he cried.

Yusuf perceived that he had to deal with a fanatic, a religious enthusiast, who would not be reasoned with.

"Yes," he continued, "may it be Mohammed's privilege to lead men back to truth, and to turn them from heathendom; to teach them to be wise as serpents, harmless as doves, and to show them how to walk with clean hands and hearts through the earth, living uprightly in the sight of all men!"

"Yet," ventured Yusuf, "did not Jesus teach something of this?"

"Jesus was great and good," said Mohammed; "he was needed

in his day upon the earth, but men have fallen away again, and Mohammed is the greatest and last, the prophet of Allah!"

The speaker's eyes were flashing; he was yet under the influence of an overpowering excitement. The color began to rush to his face, and Yusuf, fearing a return of the swoon, deemed it wise not to prolong the argument, but delivered the manuscript left by the peddler, saying:

"Read, O Mohammed, and see him who was able to restore the withered hand stretched forth in faith. Perceive him, and commit not this sacrilege."

Trusting himself to say no more, Yusuf hastily left the cavern, followed by Amzi, who remarked, thoughtfully:

"Yet, there is much good, too, in that which Mohammed would advocate."

"There is," assented Yusuf. "Yet, though I know not why, I cannot trust this man. 'Tis an instinct, if you will. What, think you, does he mean to win by this procedure,—power, or esteem, or fame?"

Amzi shook his head quickly in denial. "Mohammed is one of the most upright of men, one of the last to seek personal favor or distinction by dishonest means, one of the last to be a maker of lies. Verily, Yusuf, I know not what to think of his revelations. If he does not in truth see these visions, he at least imagines he does. He is honest in what he says."

"'If he does not in truth'!" repeated Yusuf. "Surely you, Amzi, have no confidence in his visions?"

Amzi smiled. "And yet Yusuf, no longer ago than last night, was ready to believe the testimony of a pauper Jew in regard to similar assertions," he said. "But keep your mind easy, friend; I have not accepted Mohammed's claims. I am open to conviction yet, and I am not hasty to believe. In fact, I must confess, Yusuf, an entire lack of that fervor, of that capacity for religious feeling, which is so marked a trait in my Persian priest."

"Yet you, too, professed to be a seeker for truth," said Yusuf, reproachfully.

"My desire for truth is simply to know it for the mere sake of knowing it," said Amzi.

Yusuf sighed. He did not realize that he had to deal with a peculiar nature, one of the hardest to impress in spiritual things—the indifferent, calculating mind, which is more than half satisfied with moral virtue, not realizing the infinitely higher, nobler, happier life that comes from the inspiration of a constant companionship with God.

"Alas, I am but a poor teacher, Amzi," he said. "You know, perhaps, more of the doctrines of these Christians than I; yet I am convinced that to me has come a blessing which you lack, and I would fain you had it too. And I know so little that it seems I cannot help you. You will, at least, come and talk with Nathan?"

"As you will," said Amzi, in a half bantering tone. "Prove to me that these Hebrews are infallible, and I shall half accept their Jewish philosophy."

"You cannot expect to find them or any one on this earth infallible," returned Yusuf, quietly. "I can only promise that you will find in them quiet, sincere, upright Christians."

They had reached a sudden turn on the path, and before them, on the top of a steep cliff, stood Dumah, with his fair hair streaming in the sunshine. He was singing, and they paused to listen.

> *"He is gone, the noble, the handsome,*
> *And the tears of the mother are falling*
> *Like dews from the cup of the lily*
> *When it bends its head in the darkness."*

"Poor Dumah!" said Amzi, "singing his thoughts as usual. What now, Dumah? Who is weeping?"

"A poor Jewess," said the boy, "and her two children cling to her gown and weep too. Ah, if Dumah had power he would soon set him free."

"Set whom free?" asked Yusuf.

"The father; they say he took the cup to buy bread; but for the sake of the children, Dumah would set him free."

"Oh, it is only a case of stealing down in the Jewish quarter," said Amzi, carelessly.

"Yet," returned the other, "a weeping mother and helpless children should appeal to the heart of Amzi the benevolent. Let us turn aside and see what it is about. Dumah, lead us."

They followed the boy to the hall or courtroom of the city. A judge sat on a raised dais; witnesses were below, and the owner of the gold cup was talking excitedly and calling loudly for justice.

"There is the culprit," whispered Amzi.

Yusuf was struck dumb. It was Nathan, the Christian Jew! Agony was written in his face, yet there was patience in it too. His arms were bound, and his head was bent in what might have been interpreted as humiliation.

"Once more," cried the judge, "have you aught to say for yourself, Jew?"

Nathan raised his head proudly, and looked the Judge straight in the eyes.

"I am guiltless," he said, in low, firm tones.

A murmur burst from the crowd, and exclamations could be heard.

"Not guilty! And the cup found in his house!"

"Coward dog! Will he not yet confess?"

"The scourge is too good for him!"

"Have you no explanation to offer?" asked the judge.

"None."

"Then, guards, place him in irons to await our further pleasure. In the meantime forty lashes of the scourge. Next!"

Nathan walked out with firm step and head erect. A low sob burst from some one in the crowd. It was the wife of Nathan, weeping, while little Manasseh and Mary clung to her weeping too.

Yusuf touched her on the arm. "Hush! Be calm!" he said. "All will yet be well. I, for one, know that he is innocent, and I will not rest until he is free."

"Thank God! He has not forsaken us!" exclaimed the woman.

Yusuf put a piece of money into Manasseh's hand. "Here, take your mother home, and buy some bread," he said.

"And here, pretty lad, know you the touch of gold?" said Amzi, as he slipped another coin into the child's hand. "Now, Yusuf," he went on, "come, let us see your Jewish friends of yester-even."

"Alas, Amzi, these are they," returned the priest, sadly, "and I fear yon poor woman feels little like talking to us in the freshness of her grief."

Amzi laughed, mysteriously. "So your teacher has proved but a common Jew thief," he said.

Yusuf turned almost fiercely. "Do you believe this vile story?" he exclaimed. "Did you not see truth stamped upon Nathan's face?"

"You must admit that circumstances are against him. The proof seems conclusive."

"I will never believe it, were the proof produced by their machinations ten times as conclusive! There is some mystery here which I will unravel!"

"My poor Yusuf, you are too credulous in respect to these people. So be it. You believe in your Jews, I shall believe in my

Mohammed, until the tale told is a different one," laughed Amzi; and for the moment Yusuf felt helpless.

CHAPTER VII.

YUSUF STUDIES THE
SCRIPTURES.—CONNECTING EVENTS.

"Surely an humble husbandman that serveth God is better than a proud philosopher who, neglecting himself, is occupied in studying the course of the heavens."
—Thomas á Kempis.

For many weeks, even months, after this, Yusuf's life, to one who knew not the workings of his mind, seemed colorless, and filled with a monotonous round of never varying occupation. Yet in those few weeks he lived more than in all his life before. Life is not made up of either years or actions—the development of thought and character is the important thing; and in this period of apparent waiting, Yusuf grew and developed in the light of his new understanding.

He read and thought and studied, and yet found time for paying some attention to outer affairs. In Persia he had amassed a considerable fortune, which he had conveyed to Mecca in the form of jewels sewn into his belt and into the seams of his garments, hence he was abundantly able to pay his way, and to expend something in charity; and between his and Amzi's generosity the family of Nathan lacked nothing.

Yusuf obtained possession of parts of the Scriptures, written on parchment, and spent every morning in their perusal, ever finding this period a precious feast full of comforting assurances, and hope inspiring promises. He never forgot to pray for Amzi, to whom he often read and expounded passages of Scripture, without being able to notice any apparent effect of his teaching.

It troubled him much that Amzi lent such a willing ear to Mohammed, and to the few fanatics among the Hanifs who had now professed their belief in this self proclaimed prophet of Allah. It seemed marvelous that a man of Amzi's wisdom and learning should be so carried away by such a flimsy doctrine as that which Mohammed now began to proclaim. Amzi appeared to have fallen under the spell which Mohammed seemed to cast over many of those with whom he came in contact; and, though he acknowledged no belief in the so-called prophet, neither did he profess disbelief in him.

Yusuf's happiest hours were those spent in the little Jewish

Christian church, a poor, uncomfortable building, where an earnest handful of Jews, who were nevertheless firm believers in the divinity of Christ, met, often in secret, always in fear of the derisive Arabs, for prayer and study of the Gospel. Among these, the wife of Nathan was never absent.

Yusuf sought untiringly to solve the mystery of the gold cup. Circumstantial evidence was certainly against Nathan. Awad, a rich merchant of Mecca, had placed the cup near a window in his house, and had forgotten to remove it ere retiring for the night. A short time before dawn he had heard a noise and risen to see what it was. He had gone outside just in time to see a figure passing hurriedly across a small field near his house. Even then he had not thought of the cup. But in the morning it was missed, and tracks were followed from the window as far as the ruined house to which Nathan's family had gone in their poverty. The house was searched, and the cup was found hidden in a heap of rubbish in an unused apartment.

Nathan had just returned with little save the clothes he wore; it was well known that his wife and children had been verging on starvation, and the public, ever ready to judge, formed its own conclusion, and turned with Nemesis eye upon the poor Jew.

No clue whatever remained, except a small carnelian, which Yusuf found afterwards upon the floor, and which he took possession of at once. For hours he would wander about, hoping to find some trace of the robber, who, he firmly believed, had fancied himself followed by Awad, and had hurriedly secreted the cup, trusting to return for it later, and to make his escape in the meantime.

All this, however, did not help poor Nathan, who, chained and fettered, languished in a close, poorly ventilated cell, with little hope of deliverance. Yusuf knew the rancor of the Meccans against the Jews, and somewhat feared the result, yet he did not give up hope.

"We are praying for him," Nathan's wife would say. "Nathan and Yusuf are praying too, and we know that whatever happens must be best, since God has willed it so for us."

Little Manasseh chafed more than anyone at the long suspense. One day he said:

"Mother, my name means blackness, sorrow, or something like that, does it not? Why did you call me Manasseh? Was it to be an omen of my life?"

"Forbid that it should!" the mother exclaimed, passing her hand lovingly through his waving hair. "It must have been because of your curls, black as a raven's wing. Sorrow will not be always. Joy may come soon; but if not, 'at eventide it shall be light.'"

"Does that mean in heaven?" he asked.

"He has prepared for us a mansion in the heavens, an house not made with hands. 'There shall be no night there,' and 'sorrow and sighing shall flee away,'" said the mother with a far-away look in her eyes.

"But it seems so long to wait, mother," said the boy impatiently.

"Yet heaven is not far away, Manasseh," she returned, quickly. "Heaven is wherever God is. And have we not him with us always? 'In all thy ways acknowledge him, and he shall direct thy paths.' Never forget that, Manasseh."

"Well, I wish we were a little happier now," he would say; and then, to divert the boy's attention from his present troubles, his mother would tell him about her happy home in Palestine, where she and her little sister, Lois, had watched their sheep on the green hillsides, and woven chains of flowers to put about the neck of their pet lamb; of how they grew up, and Lois married the Bedouin Musa, and had gone far away.

Thus far, Yusuf knew nothing of this connection of Nathan's family with his Bedouin friends. It was yet to prove another link in the chain which was binding him so closely to this godly family. His many occupations, and the feeling which impelled him at every spare moment to seek for some clue which would lead to Nathan's liberation, left him little time for conversation with them for the present, except to see that their wants were supplied.

Then, too, he was troubled about Amzi, and somewhat anxious about the result of Mohammed's proclamations, which were now beginning to be noised abroad. From holding meetings in caves and private houses, the "prophet" had begun to preach on the streets, and from the top of the little eminence Safa, near the foot of Abu Kubays.

Many of the people of Mecca held him up to ridicule, and treated his declarations with derisive contempt. Among his strongest opponents were his own kindred, the Koreish, of the line of Haschem and of the rival line of Abd Schems. The head of the latter tribe, Abu Sofian, Mohammed's uncle, was especially bitter. He was a formidable foe, as he lived in the highlands, his castles being built on precipitous rocks, and manned by a set of wild and savage Arabs.

Yet Mohammed went on, neither daunted by fear nor discouraged by sarcasm. The number of his followers steadily increased; his first converts, Ali, his cousin, and Zeid, his faithful servant, being quickly joined by many others.

Mohammed now boldly proclaimed the message delivered to him in the cave of Hira the Koran. He declared that the law of Moses had given way to the Gospel, and that the Gospel was now to give way to the Koran; that the Savior was a great prophet, but was not divine; and that he, Mohammed, was to be the last and greatest of all the prophets.

Such assertions were usually received with shouts of derision; and yet, when Mohammed eloquently upheld fairness and sincerity in all public and private dealings, and urged the giving of alms, and the living of a pure and humble life, there were those who, like Amzi, felt that there was something worthy of admiration in the new prophet's religion; and his very firmness and sincerity, even when spat upon, and covered with mud thrown upon him as he prayed in the Caaba, won for him friends.

The opposition of his uncles, Abu Lahab and Abu Sofian, was, however, carried on with the greatest rancor; and at last a decree was issued by Abu Sofian forbidding the tribe of the Koreish from having any intercourse whatever with Mohammed. This decree was written on parchment, and hung up in the Caaba, and Mohammed was ultimately forced to flee from the city. He and his disciples went for refuge to the ravine of Abu Taleb, at some distance from Mecca. Here they would have suffered great want, had it not been for the kindness of Amzi, who managed to send them food in secret.

But the prophet's zeal never flagged. When the Ramadhan again came round, and it was safe to venture from his temporary retreat, he came boldly into the city, preached again from the hill Safa, and proclaimed his new revelations, praying for the people, and ending every prayer with the declaration now universal throughout the Moslem world,—

"God! There is no God but he, the ever-living! He sleepeth not, neither doth he slumber! To him belong the heavens and the earth, and all that they contain. Who shall intercede with him unless by his permission? His sway extendeth over the heavens and the earth, and to sustain them both is no burthen to him. He is the High, the Mighty!"

The sublimity of this eulogy of the Most High may be readily traced to the psalms, particularly to that grandest of all songs, the one hundred and fourth psalm, which has been said to be remarkable in that it embraces the whole cosmos. And, in fact, the whole trend of the Koran may be traced to a study of the Bible, particularly to the New Testament, with occasional digressions into the Mishnu, and the Talmud of the Hebrews.

"Feed the hungry! Visit the sick! Bow not to idols! Pray constantly, and direct thy prayers immediately to the Deity!" These were the constant exhortations of the prophet during these first days of his ministry—exhortations which demand the admiration of all who consider the grossness and idolatry of the age in which he lived. Had he never gone further, succeeding ages might have been tempted to pardon his hallucinations. At the time, doctrines which savored of so much magnanimity, and which were immeasurably in advance of the mockery of religion that had so long held sway among the majority of the Arabs, at once commended themselves to many. The effect of the new teaching was enhanced by the burning enthusiasm and powerful oratory of Mohammed, who was not ignorant of the effect of eloquent delivery and glowing language on a people ever passionate and keenly susceptible to the influence of a strong and vivid presentation.

[margin handwritten note: Sounds like O'Bama]

Ridicule and persecution ceased for a time, and at last, when the decree was removed, Mohammed and his followers returned in triumph to Mecca.

Once again he was obliged to fly for his life. Accompanied by Zeid, he went to Tayf, and there spent a month in its perfumed vales, wandering by cooling streams, meditating beneath the waving fronds of the palm trees, or resting in cool gardens, lulled by the rustling leaves of the nebeck (the lotus tree), and inhaling the fresh perfume of peach and apple blooms.

But the inhabitants of Tayf grew hostile, and the prophet again set out on foot for Mecca. He sat down to rest in an orchard. There he dreamed that a host of genii waited before him, begging him to teach them El Islam.

In the night he arose and proceeded, with renewed courage, on his journey. On the way he fell in with some pilgrims from Yathrib, or Medina, and to them he unfolded his revelations. They listened spellbound as he preached from Al Akaba, and besought him that he would come or would send disciples with them to their northern town. Accordingly, Mohammed chose several converts to accompany them upon this first mission, and a time was

8   Moslems assert that upon this night Mohammed was carried through the seven heavens of which El Islam tells.

set for their going.

On the evening preceding this appointed time, Yusuf sat in a hanging balcony of Amzi's house. The pink flush of the setting sun was over the sky; the murmur of the city arose with a subdued hum—"the city's stilly sound"; a parchment containing a part of the Scriptures was on the priest's knee, but he stopped reading and gave himself up to meditation, wondering deeply at the strange course that events were taking, and surmising vaguely the probable result of the revolution that seemed impending.

His thoughts turned to Amzi, who, as yet, closed his ears to the Gospel tidings which were proving such a comfort and joy to the priest.

A step sounded behind him. It was Amzi himself, attired in traveling garb, and with his camel-stick already in his hand.

"What now, friend Yusuf? Dreaming still?" he said. "Will you not say farewell to your friend?"

"What! Are you going on a journey? Pray, where goes Amzi on such short notice?"

"Ah," smiled Amzi, "I almost fear to tell my Persian proselyte, lest the vials of his wrath be poured on my defenceless and submissive head. To make a long story short, I go with the disciples of Mohammed to Medina."

"As Mohammed's disciple? Amzi, has it come to this!" exclaimed the priest.

"Chain your choler, my friend," laughed the other. "I merely go to observe the outcome of this movement in the town of the North. Besides, the heat of Mecca in this season oppresses me, and I long for the cool breezes of Medina. Yusuf, I shall have rare letters to write you, for I feel that there will be a mighty movement in favor of Mohammed there."

"You begin to believe in him, Amzi!" said Yusuf in tones of deepest concern.

"His doctrines suit me, as containing many noble precepts. His proclamations are moving the town in such a way as was never known heretofore."

"Consider the movement caused by the teaching of Christ when he was on earth!" cried Yusuf. "Dare you compare this petty tempest with that?"

"Yet Christ's very words have been here where all might read them, for long enough. Why have they not drawn the attention of, and, if divine, why have they not shown their power among, our citizens?"

"Because ye have eyes that see not, and ears that hear not!"

cried the priest impetuously. "Can you not see that the doctrines of the Scriptures are just those which Mohammed proclaims? He seizes upon them, he gives them as his own, because he knows they are good, yet he commits the sacrilege of posing as a divine agent! Good cannot come out of this except in so far as a few precepts of the Gospel, all plagiarized as they are, exert their influence upon the lives of people."

Amzi looked inconvincible. "I grant the excellence of Gospel teaching," he said, "but your conception of God's love I cannot seem to feel, often as you have explained it to me. Mohammed's revelations appear plausible. Yet, look not so doleful, brother. Amzi has not become a Mohammedan. He is still ready to believe as soon as he can see."

"Yes, yes; like Thomas, you must see and feel ere you will believe. God grant that the seeing and feeling may not come too late!"

Amzi smiled, and passed his arm affectionately about the priest's shoulder. "What a thorn in the flesh to you is Amzi the benevolent," he said, kindly. "Notwithstanding, give me your blessing, priest. Give me credit for being, at least, honest, and bid me good speed before I go."

"Heaven forbid that aught but blessing from Yusuf should ever follow Amzi!" returned the other, warmly. "May heaven keep and direct you, my friend, my brother!"

The friends embraced, according to the custom of the land, and separated; Amzi to join the half naked pilgrims, who had not yet donned their traveling robes, Yusuf to lift his heart to Heaven, as he now did in every circumstance. In this silent talk to God he received comfort, and his heart was filled with hope for Amzi.

Even this journey, which seemed so inauspicious, might, he thought, be but the beginning of a happy end. He had learned that there are no trifles in life; that no event is so insignificant that God may not make use of it. He felt that Amzi was not utterly indifferent to the influence of divine power, so he waited in patience.

CHAPTER VIII.

WHEREIN IS TOLD THE STORY OF NATHAN'S LIBERATION.

"The winds, as at their hour of birth,
Leaning upon the ridged sea,
Breathed low around the rolling earth
With mellow preludes, 'We are free.'"
—Tennyson.

During all this time, there was no news of release for poor Nathan. In his close cell, ventilated by one little window, and, in the fetid odor of its air, he pined away. A low fever had rendered him exceedingly weak; he could not eat the wretched food of the prison; his face grew haggard, and his bones shone through the flesh with almost skeletonlike distinctness. Yet no murmur passed his lips.

From his window, set high in the wall, he could see the sun as it rose over Abu Kubays; he could catch the occasional glint of a bright wing as a dove or a swallow flitted past beneath the white sky; and he said, "God is still good, blessed be his name!"

Yet the grief of being separated from his loved ones, and the uncertainty of their welfare, preyed upon his mind, almost shaking the trust which had upheld him so long. It was a time of trial for poor Nathan, yet his faith came forth from the trial untarnished.

Yusuf sought in vain to gain admission to the poor prisoner: the utmost that he could accomplish was to pay the attendant for carrying one brief message to him, assuring him that his wife and children were well, and cared for.

The mystery of the gold cup was still unsolved. One day, however, when going down one of the busiest streets, Yusuf saw, at some distance, a little man walking along with a pack on his back. The peculiar hopping motion of his gait proclaimed him at once to be Abraham, the little Jew.

"The very man!" thought Yusuf. "If any one between Syria and Yemen can ferret out a mystery, it is Abraham the peddler. If I can once set him in earnest upon the track, deliverance may be speedy for poor Nathan."

The peddler was walking very rapidly, but Yusuf strode after him, now losing sight of him in the crowd, now catching a glimpse of his little bobbing figure, until, out of breath, he finally reached him and caught his arm.

The Jew started in surprise. "Defend us, friend!" he exclaimed. "You come on a man like the poison wind, as quickly if not as deadly. So you are still in Mecca! What are you doing now?"

He was as inquisitive as ever, but Yusuf did not resent the trait in him now.

"I am on important business just at present, my friend," he said, in his kindliest tone, "on business in which I am sure Abraham the Jew can help me, better than any other man in Mecca."

"Ha!" exclaimed the peddler, "and what may that be?"

"Can you keep a still tongue when it is necessary, Jew?"

The peddler placed his fingers on his lips, rolled up his eyes, and nodded assent.

"Then come with me to the house of Amzi the benevolent,—my Meccan home,—and I shall explain."

When seated comfortably on divans in the coolest part of the house, Yusuf told the story of the gold cup, and intimated that Abraham's wandering life and the numberless throngs of people with whom his trade threw him in contact, gave him facilities, impossible to others, of doing a little detective work in a quiet way.

The Jew listened, silent and motionless, with his eyes fixed on a lotus-bud carved on the cornice. Only once did he turn and fix his little round eyes sharply on the priest's face.

"There is just one more thing—" continued Yusuf, then he stopped. He was about to tell of the little carnelian stone, when his eye fell upon one of the numerous rings upon the Jew's fat fingers. There, in the center of it, was a small cavity from which, apparently, a jewel of some sort had fallen from its setting.

Yusuf almost sprang to his feet in the excitement of the discovery.

"Well?" asked the Jew, noting the pause.

"I will tell you later," said Yusuf. "For the present—have some dates, will you not?"

A servant entered with a tray on which were fruits and small cakes.

The peddler besought Yusuf, for friendship's sake, to eat with him; but the Persian made a gesture of disgust.

"I have already eaten," he said. "Overeating in Mecca in the hot season is not wise. Abraham, do you always wear so many rings on your fingers?"

"Oh, no," returned the Jew, "sometimes I wear them; sometimes I carry them for months in my belt. This"—pointing to a huge band of ancient workmanship—"is the most curious one of the lot. I got it for carrying a bundle of manuscript from a man at Oman to your friend Amzi, here. It seems that Amzi had once lived with him at Oman, but the man—I forget his name—went inland to Teheran, or some other place in Persia, and Amzi, after traveling about for two or three years, settled in Mecca. This one"—and he pointed out the ring on which Yusuf's eyes were fixed—"is the most expensive of the lot, but a stone fell out of it once when I was carrying it in my belt."

"Did you not look in your belt for it?"

"No use; it had worked out between the stitches. I had no idea where I lost it."

"Have you had that ring long?"

"Long! Why, that ring has not been off my person for fifteen years."

"I suppose you would not sell it?"

The peddler shrugged his shoulders, and looked up with a shrewd glance.

"That depends on how much money it would bring."

"I have little idea of the value of such rings," said the Persian, "but I have a friend who, I am convinced, would appreciate that one. I should like to present it to him. Will you take this for it?"

He drew forth a coin worth three times the value of the ring. The peddler immediately closed the bargain and handed the ring over, then devoted his attention again to the table.

The priest went to the window. He drew the little stone from his bosom and slipped it into the cavity. It fitted exactly. He then walked back to the table, and held it before the astonished Jew.

"How now, Jew?" he said with a smile. "Saw you such a gem before?"

"My very own carnelian!" exclaimed the peddler. "Where did you find it?"

"You are sure it is yours?"

"Sure! On my oath, it is mine. There is not another such stone in Arabia, with that streak across the top."

The priest laid his hand on the Jew's shoulder and bent close to him. "That stone," he said, "was found in the house of Nathan the Jew, beside the stolen cup. How came it there?"

The little Jew turned pale. His guilt showed in his face. He knew that he was undone.

With a quick, serpentlike movement, he attempted to escape, but the priest's grasp was firm as a vise.

"No, peddler!" he said, "you may go, but it must be with me. To the magistrate you must go, and that right speedily. The innocent must no longer suffer in your rightful place. Come, Aza,"—to an attendant who had been in the room—"your tongue may be needed to supplement mine."

The Jew's little eyes rolled around restlessly. He was a thorough coward, and his teeth chattered with fear as he was half dragged into the blinding glare of the street, and down the long, crooked way, with a crowd of beggars and saucy boys following in the wake of the trio. Once or twice again he made a quick and sudden movement to elude the grasp of his captors, but the priest's grip was firm and his muscle like steel. Justice was in Yusuf's heart, and his anxiety to procure Nathan's release was so great that he strode on, almost forgetting the poor little Jew, who was obliged to keep up a constant hobbling run to save himself from being dragged to the ground.

In the hall of justice the usual amount of questioning went on, but the evidence afforded by the ring was so conclusive that the order for Nathan's release and the peddler's imprisonment was soon given.

Yusuf accompanied the guards to Nathan's cell. The poor prisoner was sitting on the bare clay with his head buried on his knee. An unusual clamor sounded outside of the door. The heavy bolt was withdrawn, and the next moment Yusuf rushed in, crying, "Free, Nathan, free!"

Nathan fell on the other's bosom. The sudden joy was too much for him, and he could only lie, like a little child, sobbing on the breast of the stalwart priest.

The warden rattled the bolts impatiently. "Come, there's room outside!" he said. "I have not time to stand here all day!"

"Pardon us," said the priest, gently. "We go; yet, warden, ere we depart, may I ask you to deal leniently with that poor wretch?" and he pointed to the Jew, who was now crouched shivering in his chains.

"We but do as we are ordered," returned the warden unfeelingly. "The officers will be here presently with the scourge; we can not prevent that."

The peddler winced, and Nathan raised a face full of pity. "Warden," he said, "if you have a drop of mercy in your heart, if you hope for mercy for yourself, treat him as a man. Let him not die for want of a pittance of water."

He turned the sleeve of his loose garment back to expose the emaciated arm with the bones showing through the loose skin.

"There," he said, "let that touch your heart, if heart you have, and spare him. Poor Abraham!"—turning to the peddler—"did I not see you here, the joy of my release would be unspeakable."

But Abraham only turned to bestow a look of hate and malice upon the priest.

Then Yusuf and Nathan passed out into the pure, fresh air, now growing cool with the approach of evening. Never did air seem so pure and sweet; never did swallows twitter so gladly; never did the peak of Abu Kubays shine so gloriously in the sun; never did the voices of people sound so joyous or their faces beam so brightly.

"Come," said Nathan, "to my wife and children, that we may all return thanks together. Verily 'Many are the afflictions of the righteous, but the Lord delivereth him out of them all.' 'Blessed be God, which hath not turned away my prayer, nor his mercy from me.' 'I had fainted unless I had believed to see the goodness of the Lord in the land of the living.' 'My flesh faileth, but God is the strength of my heart, and my portion forever.'"

So, uttering exclamations from the pages of Scripture, did the devout Jew pass onward to his home, which was once more filled with "joy and gladness, thanksgiving and the voice of melody." Before leaving, Yusuf presented him with the ring containing the little stone, as a memento of his deliverance.

And Abraham? He received the full weight of the scourge; and may we be pardoned in anticipating, and say that for two days he lay nursing his wrath and his wounds; but, on the third day after his imprisonment, his agility suddenly returned. He managed in some inexplicable way known only to himself to work free of his fetters, and when the keeper came with food in the evening, blinded by the dim light of the cell, he did not perceive the little peddler crouched in a heap in the middle of the floor.

Scarcely was the door opened when the Jew bounced like a ball past the keeper's feet, almost upsetting him; then, darting like an arrow between the astonished guards without, he was off. A hue and cry was raised, but the little peddler had disappeared as completely as if the earth had opened up and swallowed him.

CHAPTER IX.

AMZI AT MEDINA.

"With half shut eyes ever to seem
Falling asleep in a half dream!
To dream and dream like yonder amber light
Which will not leave the myrrh-bush on the height."
                                   —Tennyson.

Without entering into detail it may be briefly stated that the success of Mohammed's disciples in Medina was simply marvelous. Converts joined them every day, while those who were not prepared to believe in the Meccan's divine mission were at least anxious to see and hear the prophet.

Amzi did no work in behalf of the new religion. He was simply an onlooker, though not an unsympathetic one; and, it must be confessed, he spent most of his time in that voluptuous do-nothingness in which the wealthy Oriental dreams away so much of his time,—sitting or reclining on perfumed cushions, a fan in his hand and a long pipe at his mouth, too languid, too listless, even to talk; listening to the soft murmur of Nature's music, the nightwind sighing through the trees beneath a star-gemmed sky, the song of a solitary bulbul warbling plaintively among the myrtle and oleander blooms, the plash of a fountain rippling near with "a sound as of a hidden brook in the leafy month of June"; this, the exquisite languor of the East, "for which the speech of England has no name," the "Kaif" of the Arab, the drowsy falseness of the Lotos-eaters' ideal:

"Death is the end of life; ah, why
Should life all labor be?
Let us alone."

And so the months went by, until at last a band of emissaries, to the number of seventy, was appointed to take a journey to Mecca for the purpose of meeting with Mohammed and discussing with him the advisability of his taking up his residence at Medina.

A herald brought news of this embassy to the prophet. He went forth to meet them, and Yusuf, hearing by chance of the appointed conference, set out posthaste after Mohammed's party, eager to get even a pressure of the hand from Amzi, his heart's brother, who he felt sure would accompany the emissaries. In order to overtake them more quickly, he proceeded with a trusty guide by a shorter route across the hills.

The night was exceptionally dark, and even the guide became confused. The way led on and on between the interminable hills, until the two in complete uncertainty reined their steeds on the verge of a cliff that seemed to overhang a deep and narrow basin, bounded by flinty rock which even in the darkness loomed doubly black, and which rang beneath the horses' feet with that peculiar, metallic sound that proclaimed it black basalt, the "hell-stone" of the Arabs.

It was indeed an eerie spot. A thick fringe of thorny shrubs grew along the edge of the cliff; at intervals yawned deep fissures, across which the wise little Arabian ponies stepped gingerly; and above, outlined in intense black against the dark sky, were numerous peaks and pinnacles and castellated summits, such as the Arabs love to people with all manner of genii and evil spirits of the waste and silent wilderness. It was a spot likely to be infested with robbers, and Yusuf and his guide waited in some trepidation while considering what to do.

Presently a dull trampling sounded in the distance. It came nearer and nearer, and the two lone wanderers on the cliff scarcely dared to breathe.

The tread of camels was soon discernible, the "Ikh! Ikh!" (the sound used to make camels kneel) of the camel drivers rising from the dark pass below to the ears of the men above. Apparently the party was about to make a halt in the dark basin; and should it prove to be a band of hill-robbers, Yusuf and his companion were in a precarious position, for the slightest sound made by them or their ponies would probably prove the signal for an onslaught; but by patting and quieting the animals, they managed to keep their restlessness in check and so waited, scarcely knowing what to do next.

Ere ten minutes had elapsed, however, the tread of camels was again heard, and another party came in from the opposite direction, halting at the other end of the ravine. A call was sounded and at once answered by the body immediately below. The newcomers advanced, and mutual recognitions seemed to take place, although Yusuf could distinguish neither the voices nor the words.

The parties were, in reality, those of Mohammed and the emissaries of Medina, who at once opened negotiations. After the salutations were over, they extended to Mohammed a formal invitation to Medina.

"We will receive you as a confederate, obey you as a leader, and defend you to the last extremity, even as we defend our wives and children," said the spokesman.

"For your gracious invitation accept my most hearty thanks," said Mohammed. "My work is not yet ended in Mecca, yet ere long I hope to pay at least a visit to you, O believers of Medina."

"But," said the leader, "if you are recalled to your own district you will not forsake us?"

"All things," replied Mohammed, "are now common between us. Your blood is my blood. Your ruin is my ruin. We are bound to each other by the ties of honor and interest. I am your friend and the enemy of your foes."

He then chose twelve of the men to be the especial heralds of his faith, and all, placing their hands in his, swore fealty to him in life and in death.

"If we are killed in your service, what shall be our reward?" asked one of the number.

"Paradise!" cried the prophet. "Vales of eternal rest and felicity, odors of sweet spices on the air, blessed spirits to—"

"Hold!" cried a voice from the air above. "Who are you, Mohammed, who can dare to promise that which belongs to the Creator alone? Impostor, take heed!"

It was only Yusuf, who, in his anxiety to discover if the gloomy vale were indeed the nest of some daring mountain chief, had noiselessly descended to an overhanging ledge, and had heard the last confident assertion of the prophet.

But the utmost consternation fell upon the Arabs below. Some, believing the voice to be that of a demon of the rock, were seized with sudden panic; others shouted excitedly, "Spies! spies!" and the assembly broke up in confusion, all scurrying off, leaving Yusuf and his guide again alone on the rock.

"Amzi! Amzi!" shouted the priest, with a forlorn hope that his friend might have lingered behind the fleeing party; but the only response was the beat of hoofs flying in every direction, and the dull thud of the camels' padded feet. There was nothing better to be done than wait until morning, so Yusuf and the guide lay down on the hard rock for the rest of the night.

For some time after this affairs seemed to be at a standstill. Mohammed still continued to preach, now from the hill Safa, now from the knoll El Akaba at the north of the town.

His wife, Cadijah, had died some time before, and he had

since married a widow, Sawda, and become betrothed to a child, Ayesha, the daughter of his friend and disciple, Abu Beker.

But events in Mecca were fast hastening to a crisis. Abu Sofian, still the most mortal enemy to Mohammed and his religion, had succeeded Abu Taleb in the government of Mecca, and no sooner had he become head of the state than he determined to crush Mohammed, and exterminate his religion at any cost. A plot for the assassination of the prophet was formed. Several of the tribe of the Koreish and their allies were appointed to kill Mohammed, in order to avert the blood-revenge of Mohammed's immediate kin, the Haschemites, who, it was thought, would not dare to avenge themselves upon such numerous and such scattered foes.

The attack was planned with the utmost secrecy in the cellar of a house, and at a time but the space of three hours before daybreak, when all Mecca lay chained in slumber.

Yet not all. Abraham, the Jew, was, as usual, on the alert. Since his escape he had been prowling about the hills, penniless, and hence unable to leave the district. He had now come down to steal food, for necessity, in his eyes, rendered any such proceeding pardonable; and, perceiving a mysterious light issuing from a chink in the wall, his natural curiosity asserted itself. He lay down flat on the ground, put his ear to the chink, and succeeded in hearing every word of the plot.

Here, then, was a chance to gain favor and protection from at least a few in Mecca. He would disclose the plot to Mohammed and his vizier, and beseech their protection as the price of his services as a savior of the prophet's life. Accordingly, a couple of hours before the time appointed for the assassination, and as soon as the cover of darkness rendered his own appearance in the city safe, he hastened to the prophet.

No time was to be lost. Mohammed, accompanied by Abu Beker and the Jew, at once fled; while Ali, to deceive the spies, and keep them as long as possible in check, wrapped himself in the prophet's green cloak, moved round with it on for some time, and at last lay down on Mohammed's bed.

When the assassins entered, intending to rush upon the sleeping form and destroy it, Ali threw the cloak off and sat up. In the meantime the fugitives had reached the cave of Thor, three miles distant, from whence, after three days, they escaped to Medina.

This was the famous flight of the prophet, the Hegira, or

Hejra, in the year 622 A.D. and about the fifty-third year of Mohammed's age.

CHAPTER X.

MOHAMMED'S ENTRANCE INTO MEDINA.

"Oh, it is excellent
To have a giant's strength: but it is tyrannous
To use it like a giant."
—Shakespeare.

Once more after the lapse of years let us look at Amzi as he sat one morning in his house at Medina.

The cool and pleasant atmosphere of the town in contrast with the burning, breathless heat of Mecca had charmed him. He had immediately purchased a house and furnished it with the luxurious splendor which suited his rather voluptuous taste.

The apartment in which he sat was in the middle story, the one sacred to the men in a house of Medina. Rich Persian carpets were on the floor, rugs of Inde were scattered about and piled with cushions filled with softest down. Low divans invited repose, and heavy curtains of yellow silk shut out the too bright glare of day. The ceiling, after the Persian fashion, was inlaid with mirrors, fitted in in different patterns, and divided by carved sticks of palm, stained red; and the sweet odor of richest perfumes of Arabia-Felix spread through the room as if emanating from the silken hangings of the wall.

The window was open, and the breeze from the east, bearing, as it were, tales of the Nejd, the land of brave men and beautiful women, swayed the curtains softly. Outside, in the sloping garden, waved the graceful branches of the tamarisk, glittering with dew in the early morning sun; and near the window a jujube tree stretched its dark, shining leaves and yellow fruit temptingly near. Acacias with sweet-scented yellow blossoms, oleanders glowing with rosy bloom, and a thicket of silver-leaved castors separated the little plot from the gardens below, where grew gourds and cucumbers, lime and fig trees, grape vines, watermelons and pomegranates; and beyond that lay a bright patch of Bursim, or Egyptian clover, like a yellow-green island on a darker sea.

Amzi, comfortably habited in a jubbeh of pink silk, worn over a caftan of fine white silk flowered with green and confined by a fringed, yellow sash at the waist, reclined in a position of luxurious ease at the window. Between his plump fingers he held the amber stem of a handsomely carved pipe. He looked scarcely older than when on that memorable journey in which he first met Yusuf. His eye was still as bright, his hair scarcely more gray, and his cheek as ruddy as then; yet there was a somewhat discontented look on his face.

His eye wandered over the rich garden before him, and he thought of barren, ashen Mecca. Then he looked restlessly back over the landscape below. Surely it was fair enough to calm a restless spirit.

Immediately before, and to the eastward, the sun had risen out of a mass of lilac and rose-colored cloud. The tufted trees on the distant hills stood black and distinct against the splendor of the sky. To the right the date-groves of Kuba, famed throughout Arabia, struggled through a sea of mist that piled and surged in waves of amber and purple, leaving the tree tops like islands on a vapory sea. To the left the seared and scoriæ-covered crest of Mount Ohod rose, dark and scowling, like a grim sentinel on the borders of an Elysian valley. In the rear lay the plain of El Munakhah, and the rush of the torrent El Sayh was borne on the breeze, bearing the willing mind beyond to the cool groves of Kuba, whence this raging flood dispersed itself in gentle rills, or was carried in silent channels to turn the water-wheels, or to fall, with musical plash, into wooden troughs that lay deep in the shade.

The ripple of water,—ah, what it means to Arabian ears! Little wonder that the inhabitant of the desert land never omits it from his idea of paradise, save in his conception of the highest heaven,—a conception not lacking in sublimity—that of a silent looking upon the face of God.

In the immediate foreground lay El Medina itself, with its narrow streets, its busy bazars, its fair-skinned people, and its low, yellow, flat-roofed houses, each with its well and courtyard, nestling cozily among the feathery-fronded date trees.

From the Eastern Road, a caravan from the Nejd was descending slowly into the town, and so clear was the atmosphere that Amzi could distinguish the huge, white dromedaries, and catch an occasional glint of a green shugduf, or the gorgeous litter of a grandee, trapped in scarlet and gold.

It was indeed a fair scene, and Amzi enjoyed it to the full with the keen enjoyment of one who possesses an esthetic temperament, an intense love of the beautiful. Yet he began to feel lonely in this town of his adoption. It was long since he had seen Yusuf, and he commenced to think seriously of returning for a time to Mecca.

Besides, he was tired of waiting for Mohammed's long deferred visit, and he was anxious again to see the man whose strange fascination over him he scarcely dared to acknowledge even to himself. The emptiness and idleness of his own life was beginning to pall upon him, and he compared unfavorably his sluggish existence with the busy, quietly energetic way in which Yusuf was spending his days.

One source of unfailing pleasure to him had been the companionship of Dumah, who had followed him to Medina, but was wandering about as usual, returning to Amzi when tired or hungry, as a birdling returns to its mother's wing.

And Amzi had almost a mother's love for the boy, for poor Dumah seemed a child still; he had grown but little, his face was paler than of old, his eyes were as large and blue, and his bright hair fell in the same soft curls above his regular and clear-cut features. Like Yusuf, Amzi felt that the orphan's very helplessness was an appeal to his heart, and he did not lock its doors.

Dumah now came in wearily. He lay down at Amzi's feet and put his head on his knee. The Meccan stroked his soft hair gently.

"Where has my Dumah been?" he asked tenderly.

"Watching the people going out foolishly. Dumah would not go with them."

"Going where, lad?"

"Out to the gardens where the lotus blows, and the date palms wave, and the citron and orange grow."

"And why go they, then, foolishly?" smiled Amzi.

"Because they go to meet him, and they are carrying white robes, and they will bring him in as a prince,—the wicked one, who would place himself above our blessed Master!"

Amzi started up quickly, and threw his pipe down.

"Is Mohammed here?" he cried.

"He is here. But you will not go too, Amzi? Alas that I told you! The angels I see in my dreams do not smile, they look away and vanish when I think of Mohammed. Yusuf does not love him! Let not Amzi!" pleaded the orphan.

But the Meccan was gone. Hastening on towards the outskirts of the city, he met a great crowd of people, pressing about Mohammed and Abu Beker, each of whom was dressed in a white garment, and riding triumphantly upon a white camel, the prophet being mounted on his own beast El Kaswa.

The little peddler, assigning himself a lower place, rode behind on a packmule.

Mohammed had come, and was, from the very beginning, a monarch, surrounded by an army of blind devotees, believers in his holy mission, and slavishly obedient to his will.

Amzi took the prophet to his house, and there entertained him as a respected Meccan friend, until Mohammed's home was erected. It was at Amzi's house, too, that the nuptials of Mohammed and the beautiful Ayesha, also those of Ali and the prophet's daughter Fatimah, took place.

One of Mohammed's first acts was to have a mosque built, and, from it, morning and night the call to prayers was given:

"God is great! There is no God but God! Mohammed is the prophet of God! Come to prayers. Come to prayers! God is great!"

And from this mosque Mohammed exhorted with wondrous eloquence, the music of his voice falling like a spell on the multitudes, as they listened to teachings new and more living than the old, dead, superstitious idolatry to which they were in bondage; yet, had they known it, teachings whose choicest gems were but crumbs borrowed from the words of One who had preached in all meekness and love on the shores of Galilee and the hills of Palestine more than six hundred years before.

They listened in wonder to condemnation of their belief in polytheism.

"In the name of the most merciful God," Mohammed would say, "say God is one God, the Eternal God; he begetteth not, neither is he begotten, and there is not anyone like unto him!" Thus did he aim at the foundation of Christianity, seeking to overthrow belief in the "only begotten Son of God" as a divine factor of the Trinity. Jesus he recognized as a prophet, not as God's own Son; and, while he borrowed incessantly from the Scriptures, he refused to accept them, declaring that they had become perverted, and that the original Koran was a volume of Paradise, from which Gabriel rendered him transcripts, and was, therefore, the true word of God which had been laid from time everlasting on what he called the "preserved table," close to the throne of God in the highest heaven.

And yet, during the greater part of his career, the utterances of this strange, incomprehensible man were characterized by a seemingly real glow of philanthropy and an earnest solicitude for the salvation of his countrymen from the depths of moral and spiritual degradation into which they had fallen. A missionary spirit seemed to be in him, in strange contrast and incompatibility with the sacrilegious words that often fell from his lips.

In all the records of history there is nothing more wonderful than the marvelous success which attended Mohammed at Medina. Staid and sober merchantmen, men with gray heads, fiery youths, proselytes from the tribes of the desert, even women, flocked to him every day; and he soon realized that he had a vast army of converts ready to live or die for him, ready to fight for him until the last.

Amzi, alone, of all his followers, seemed to stand aloof, half believing, yet unwilling to proclaim his belief openly; simply waiting, as he had waited all his life, to see the truth, yet too indolent to set out bravely in the quest. He preferred to look on from aside; to weigh and calculate motives, actions and results; to judge men by their fruits, though the doing so called for long waiting.

Yet Amzi grew more and more dissatisfied. He felt, though he knew not its cause, the want of a rich spiritual life, that empty hollowness which pleasures of the world and the mere consciousness of a moral life cannot satisfy.

More than once he was tempted to declare himself a follower of the prophet, but he put it off until a riper season.

Poor Dumah noted Amzi's frequent visits to the mosque with a vague dread. He had an instinctive dislike of Mohammed, whose assumptions of superiority to Jesus he understood in a hazy way, and resented with all his might.

One day he entered with a tablet of soft stone to which a cord was attached. Putting the cord about Amzi's neck, he said:

"Amzi, promise your Dumah that you will wear this always, will you not? Because Dumah might die, and could not say the words any more. Promise me!"

"I promise you," smiled Amzi, and Dumah left the room contented.

Amzi turned the tablet over, and read the familiar words traced upon the soft stone,—the words recognized as the cornerstone of Christianity:

"God so loved the world, that he gave his only begotten Son, that whosoever believeth in him should not perish, but have everlasting life."

Amzi smiled, and put the tablet in his bosom.

CHAPTER XI.

MOHAMMED BECOMES INTOLERANT.—WAR.

"Our virtues disappear when put in competition with our interests, as rivers lose themselves in the ocean."
—La Rochefoucauld.

Thirteen years had now passed since Mohammed first began to meditate in the Cave of Hira. During all that time he had preached peace, love and gentleness. With power, however, came a change in his opinions. He became not only pastor of his flock, and judge of the people, but also commander of an army. Worldly ambition took possession of his breast, and the voice of him who had cried, "Follow the religion of Abraham, who was orthodox and was no idolater. Invite men unto the way of the Lord by wisdom and mild exhortation . . . . Bear opposition with patience, but thy patience shall not be practicable unless with God's assistance. And be not thou grieved on account of the unbelievers. Let there be no violence in religion,"—now began to call, "War is enjoined you against the infidels. Fight therefore against the friends of Satan, for the stratagem of Satan is weak. And when the months wherein ye shall not be allowed to attack them be past, kill the idolaters wherever ye shall find them, and besiege them, and lay wait for them in every convenient place. Verily God hath purchased of the true believers their souls and their substance, promising them the enjoyment of Paradise on condition that they fight for the cause of God. Whether they slay or be slain, the promise for the same is assuredly due by the law, and the Gospel, and the Koran."

Clemency, he claimed, had been the instrument of Moses; wisdom, that of Solomon; righteousness, that of Christ; and now the sword was to be the instrument of Mohammed.

"The sword," he exclaimed, with flashing eye, "is the key of heaven and hell. All who draw it in the cause of the faith will be rewarded with temporal advantages; every drop shed of their blood, every peril endured by them, will be registered on high as more meritorious than fasting or prayer. If they fall in battle, their sins will at once be blotted out, and they will be transported to paradise!"

This fierce, intolerant spirit took possession of Mohammed almost from his entrance into Medina. Chapter after chapter of the Koran was produced, breathing the same bloodthirsty, implacable hatred of opposition. Mohammed, in fact, seemed like one possessed in his enthusiasm, but his doctrines caught the fancy of the wild, impressionable Arabs, who flocked to him in crowds as his fame spread throughout the length and breadth of El Hejaz, throughout the Nejd, and even to the extremities of Arabia-Felix.

And now the bloody cloud of war hovered over the peninsula, and the people trembled.

The following letter from Amzi will describe the outbreak.

From Amzi the Meccan, at Medina,
To Yusuf the priest, Mecca.

My Dear Yusuf:—

I can scarcely describe the emotions with which I write you again after a six months' interval. Affairs here in Medina have taken such an unlooked-for turn that I scarcely know what to think or what to do.

Of Mohammed's wonderful progress, you have, of course, heard. You should see him now, my dear Yusuf,—Mohammed, the peaceful trader, the devout hermit, now little less than monarch, with all the sway assumed by the most powerful despot; and yet those over whom he wields his despotism are but too willing servants, ready to say as he says, and to give their dearest heart's blood in his cause.

Indeed I know not what the outcome of it all will be. What astonishes me most is that Mohammed has suddenly assumed an aggressive attitude. Fire and the sword seem to be the watchword of him whom we knew as the gentle husband of Cadijah, the mild preacher who bowed his head and reviled not even when assailed with mud and filth in the Caaba.

Needless to say, Yusuf, I am disappointed in him. You will be only too glad to hear that. I hear that you have been exhorting the people in Mecca to pay no heed to him; that you have been seeking to promulgate your Hebrew faith, or rather the faith of your Hebrew friend, of whose innocence and release I was glad to hear.

My brother, I pride in your courage, and in the strength of

9   The initial "A" is placed at the top of all Arabian writings. It is the initial of "Allah" and the first letter of the alphabet, and is symbolic of the origin of creation.

your principles; yet, Yusuf, I beseech of you, be careful what you do or say, lest you draw down upon your head a storm of fury which you little expect. You have no idea of the revolution of feeling here in Mohammed's favor, and of the fanatic zeal of many of his followers. Be not too bold. You cannot cope singlehanded with such an overwhelming tide.

The past month, as you know, was the holy month Radjab, in which, as in the month of Ramadhan, throughout all El Hejaz, life should be held sacred, and no act of violence committed. Can you believe it when I tell you that the prophet's men have attacked more than one caravan of quiet traders and pilgrims upon their way to or from Mecca? Such a sacrilege seems unpardonable in Arab eyes, but, forsooth, the prophet has been favored with another revelation justifying him in what he has done.

This, more than aught else, makes me wonder. You, Yusuf, know what a lover of peace I have been; how it has ever grieved me to see even a butterfly fluttering along the ground with a crushed wing. Judge, then, of my horror, when I went out to the scene of the pillage and saw men lying, some dead, with ghastly faces glaring up at the hot sun, others with gaping wounds, and others moaning pitifully on the roadway, with sand on their faces and in their hair. Yusuf, it made me sick to see it. Had they been slain in fair battle I could have borne it better. Yet I was enabled to give the poor wounded creatures some water, all warm as it was from being carried so long a distance; and some of them I had conveyed to my house, so that every bedchamber has been turned into a sickroom, and your friend Amzi has been suddenly metamorphosed into a sick-nurse. Does that astonish you?

Yet, Yusuf, though I get little sleep any night, and have to be on my feet much during the day, I can assure you that I was never so happy in my life before. The constant occupation, and the sense of being able to render the poor creatures a little ease, is just what I need at present to keep me from growing moody.

The other day I saw some one who knows of you—Uzza, the Oman Arab. How or why he has come here I know not; but he is one of Mohammed's most devoted followers. For your sake, I hope you may not meet him in Medina.

I knew him, years ago, at Oman, and had letters from him for a time after he went to Persia. Perhaps that will read you the riddle as to how I knew so much of your past history, my priest. Recognizing your name, and noting your priestly bearing, it was an easy matter to connect you with the Guebre

Yusuf, of whom I had heard.

I am convinced that you are looking after my Meccan affairs as closely as possible, yet remember that Amzi has a house in Medina, too, which has ever a door open for you.

Dumah sends his love. The poor lad is greatly excited over the stirring events which are the talk of the town here.

Commend me to your friend Nathan and his family. Trusting to see or to hear from you soon,

And the peace,

Amzi.

To this letter Yusuf returned the following answer:

Yusuf, at Mecca,
To Amzi the Benevolent, Medina.

My Heart's Brother:—

Your most welcome letter lies before me, and it is quite unnecessary to say with what mingled feelings of pleasure and pain I read it,—pleasure, because, whether you will it or not, your confidence in this false prophet is tottering; pain, because of the marvelous power which this Mohammed seems to be wielding over your excitable Arab populace. Strange, indeed, is his new attitude; we had not deemed him possessed of a martial spirit; yet may we hope that this procedure will be but as the stone which shall crush his ends, falling upon his own head.

It is possible that I may be in Medina ere long. I am impatient to see you and our poor Dumah again.

And so Uzza is there, too, to bring up afresh the darkest page of my history; for Amzi, it was I, in my fanatic zeal, who induced the Persian grandmother to give up his child for sacrifice. Scarcely was it over when, even in my heathen darkness, my whole soul revolted against what I had done, and against the faith which had sanctioned such deeds of blood. It was then that I began to think and strive against the mists of darkness, until at last I fought away from the creed of my country.

I fear not to meet Uzza, although I know that he bears me no good will, and would not refrain from the assassin's knife did it satisfy his wish for blood-revenge.

Our friend, Nathan, and his family are well. Did I tell you that they have gone to live near Tayf?

I spent a pleasant day with them not long ago. They have a little cabin in the mountains, and Nathan has a few flocks which he herds out on the green hillsides. They are all so happy, and so contented with their pastoral mode of living that they think of moving back into Palestina, as the pasturage is better there. It will be a long journey, but, with the consciousness of the Father's care over them, and the bond of love to shorten the way, they will not mind it. Nathan's wife, in particular, is anxious to return to her childhood's home, and never wearies of telling her children stories of her girlhood days, when she and her sister, whom she still loves passionately, watched their sheep on the hills of Hebron.

Mary and Manasseh have grown quite tall. Manasseh is almost a man, fiery and impetuous as ever, yet wise beyond his years, and a devout Christian.

Nathan is very happy. After all his trials he has perfect rest. His face almost beamed when he said to me in the words of the Psalmist, "Unless the Lord had been my help, my soul had almost dwelt in silence. When I said, My foot slippeth, thy mercy, O Lord, held me up. For the Lord is my defence, and my God is the rock of my refuge."

He is very anxious about the hostile attitude which Mohammed has taken. "God grant," he said, "that there may not be another season of persecution. If there be, and the Lord will, I shall stay at Medina to comfort, if I may, my poor brethren there. 'Blessed are they which are persecuted for righteousness' sake, for theirs is the kingdom of heaven.' God grant that we may all be imbued with the spirit of him who said, 'Love your enemies, bless them that curse you, do good to them that hate you, and pray for them that despitefully use you.' Yet, Yusuf, it may be that we shall be forced to defend our lives, and those of our wives and children,—God knoweth. He will direct us, if we permit him, so that, living or dying, it shall be well with us."

Is not such love, such comfort in the help and presence and sympathy of God, worth more, infinitely more, than power or wealth or worldly pleasure? Nothing that happens can overwhelm this happy family, for they have the consciousness of God's love and care in all. They have Jesus for a personal friend. Amzi, what would I not give to know that you felt as they do, and as I learn to feel, more and more, every day.

My friend, I could keep on in this strain for the whole night; but I am weary, for today I talked for many hours with some of those who are half apostatizing to Mohammed.

So, Mizpah; and may the blessing of God be upon you.

Yusuf.

CHAPTER XII.

WHEREIN THE BEDOUIN YOUTH KEDAR BECOMES A MOSLEM.

"Mine honor is my life: both grow in one;
Take honor from me, and my life is done."
— Shakespeare.

The scene again opens far to the north of the Nejd, El Shark, or the East. Into one of its most favored spots, a green and secluded valley, surrounded by grassy slopes, the sun shone with the fresh brightness of early morning, sending floods of green-gold light through the leaves Of the acacias, now covered with yellowish blossoms heavy with perfume.

By the side of a little torrent, rose the black tents of a Bedouin encampment. Flocks were on the hillside, and the tinkling of the camel bells and soft bleat of the lambs sounded faintly from the distance.

At the head of the valley, upon a rounded boulder of granite sat a woman; and before her stood a young man to whom she was earnestly talking, at times stretching out her hands as though she were beseeching him for some favor.

The woman was tall and well-built, her eyes were large and dark, and their brilliancy increased, according to Bedouin custom, by the application of kohl to the lids. Her face was keen and intelligent, and her hair, braided in innumerable small plaits, and surmounted by a much bespangled headdress, was slightly streaked with gray.

The youth was slight and agile, his every movement full of grace. His face was oval, regular in its contour, and full of expression, although the Jewish cast of his features had traces of Arab blood. He seemed to be in some excitement, for, with a trait peculiar to Bedouins, his restless and deep-set eyes were now half closed until but a narrow, glittering line appeared, and now suddenly opened to their fullest extent and turned directly upon the woman to whom he talked.

"Would you have me branded among the whole tribe as a coward, mother?" he was saying. "Are not the Bedouin lads from all over the Nejd flocking to the field, even as the sparrows flock before the storm clouds of the north? And will the son of Musa be the craven, crouching at home in his mother's nest?"

"A flock of vultures are they, rather!" she cried passionately—"Vultures flocking to a feast of blood, to gloat over the carrion of brothers, sons, and husbands, left dead on the reeking plain, while in their solitary homes the women moan, even as moans the bird of the tamarisk, robbed of its young."

"'Tis your Jewish heart speaks now, mother. Ah, but your Jewish women are too soft-hearted! Know you not that Bedouin mothers have not only sent their sons to battle, but have gone themselves and fought in the thickest of the fray?"

"Ah, you are a true Bedouin, and ashamed of your mother!" returned Lois, with a sigh. "Truly, a Jewess has no place among the tribes of the wilderness."

The youth's face softened. "I am not ashamed of my mother!" he said, quickly. "But my blood leaps for the glory of battle, for the clash of cymbals, the speed of the charge, the tumult, and the victory!"

"But a hollow glory you will find it," she said scornfully. "Murder and pillage,—and all sanctioned in the name of religion!"

"Even so, is not the name of harami (brigand) accounted honorable among the desert tribes?" asked the youth, quickly.

"Alas, yes. Ye reck not that it has been said, 'Thou shalt not steal.' But you, Kedar, care not for the Jewish Scripture. Why need I quote it to you."

"Arabian religion, Arabian honor, for the Arab, say I!" returned the youth haughtily. "Let me roam over the wild on my steed, racing with the breeze, lance in hand, bound for the hunt or fray; let me swoop upon the cowardly caravans whose hundreds shriek and scream and fall back before a handful of Bedouin lads, if I will. More honorable it is to me than to plod along in a shugduf on a long-legged camel with a bag of corn or a trifle of cloth to look after. Be the Jew if you will, but give me the leaping blood, the soaring spirit of the Bedouin!"

The woman sighed again. "You will be killed, Kedar," she said. "Then what will all this profit you?"

"To die on the field is more glorious than to breathe one's life out tamely in bed," replied the other.

There was no use of reasoning with this rash youth.

"And think you this Mohammed is worthy of your sacrifice?" she asked.

"If he be really inspired, as hundreds now believe, is he not worthy of every sacrifice? Does he not promise his followers an eternal felicity?"

"A vile impostor!" exclaimed the woman harshly. "Yet you will not believe what I say, until your own eyes see and your own ears hear! Go! Go! I shall talk no more to you! If you fall it shall be no fault of Lois'!"

She arose and waved him off with an impatient gesture. Yet he lingered.

"You will forgive me, mother?" he asked, gently.

The woman's mother-heart welled to the brim. She answered brokenly:

"My son, my son! Could I do aught else? Take my blessing with you! And now, here comes your father."

Musa was feebler than upon that first night when he met Yusuf in his tent, and his hair had become almost white, yet there was the same dignity in his appearance.

"Go, Kedar," he said, "and prove that you are indeed the son of Musa. Go, and see that you bring back good news of battle!"

Kedar bent his head in token of assent.

Before an hour had passed he was mounted on the swiftest of his father's horses—a short, fleshless animal, with legs thin and of steellike muscle. But its slender neck, its small, snakelike head, its dilating nostrils, through which the light shone crimson, and its fiery, intelligent eye, showed its blood as it pawed the ground and neighed impatiently. A noble animal and a noble rider they looked as they were off like an arrow, Kedar's fine figure swaying with the movement of the steed as though rider and horse were one.

All alone went the youth across hill and valley, over rock and torrent, fearless and swift as an eagle; for Kedar scorned to seek the protection of numbers, although quite aware of the fact that a large caravan, under Abu Sofian, was even then on its way from Syria to Mecca, and was within three hours' journey from him.

CHAPTER XIII.

ABU SOFIAN'S CARAVAN.

While Kedar was thus speeding towards Medina, the caravan was also proceeding more slowly towards the south. It consisted of thirty horsemen and one thousand camels richly laden with grain, with spices, with purple of Syria, richest cloths of Damascus, and choicest perfumes of the northern regions.

It was the month Ramadhan, and the peaceful traders went confidently and securely on their way, well pleased with the success of their journey and hopeful in anticipation of the large gain they were to make during the great bazar of the pilgrimage.

While thus proceeding leisurely on, the leaders were somewhat surprised to see a solitary rider coming towards them in the greatest haste. He was mounted on a swift dromedary, and with head bent down so that his turban concealed his face, he kept striking the animal with his short camel-stick and urging it on with his shrill "Yákh! Yákh!"

All breathless he at last reached the caravan. "Is Abu Sofian here?" he cried.

"I am Abu Sofian," said the sturdy old chief. "What do you desire of me?"

"I have been sent by Amzi the benevolent," returned the other. "He bids me say to Abu Sofian that it will be well for the caravan to advance with the greatest caution, as Mohammed and his forces are in ambush on the way."

"What guarantee have I," said Abu Sofian, "that you are truly from Amzi the Meccan, and not an emissary of Mohammed sent to entrap us into some narrow glen?"

"Here is your guarantee," replied the stranger, stretching forth his hand. "Recognize you not this ring?"

"It is well," answered Abu Sofian, satisfied. "We are much beholden to you and to our friend Amzi, who we had feared was but too good a friend to this same Mohammed."

"Can you trust Amzi?" asked one near, anxiously.

"As my own soul," returned the leader. "Amzi's heart is gold; Amzi's words are jewels of purest luster. He speaks truth." Then to the messenger, "Know you what route Mohammed will take?"

"I know not. He has, doubtless, spies, who will inform him of your movements, and thus enable him to act accordingly."

"Then it remains for us to meet him by his own tactics," said

Abu Sofian, "and no time is to be lost. You, Omair my faithful, speed to Mecca with what dispatch you may. Go by the bypaths which you know so well. Tell Abu Jahl, whom I have left in charge, to send us help quickly."

Omair made obeisance and left at once.

"You, Akab and Zimmah," continued the leader, "go by the hills ahead and find out what you can. As for us, we will keep our lips closed and our eyes and ears open. Abu Sofian is not yet so old that he has forgotten the signs of the wilderness."

The vast procession moved on again slowly and in a dead silence, broken only by the trampling of the beasts and the moans of the camels.

Presently, on coming near a spot which might be deemed hazardous ground, Abu Sofian ordered a halt and went forward himself, alone and on foot. With eye on the alert, ear on a tension to catch the slightest sound, and body bent downward to facilitate the closest scrutiny of the ground, the keen old man proceeded slowly, stepping with catlike precision and quietness.

Suddenly he uttered an exclamation. A small object lay dark on the yellow sand. He picked it up. It was a date-stone. He examined it closely. It was slightly smaller than the stones of the ordinary fruit.

"A Medina date!" he exclaimed; "whoever has thrown it there!"

Going a few paces further, he found several similar ones thrown by the wayside. The trampling of the sand, too, showed that a considerable force had been on the road at no distant time.

He bent down again and directed his keen scrutiny on the road, then retraced his steps for a short distance. There were tracks pointing in both directions, but at one point the company seemed to have turned.

It was clear, then, that for some reason the force had been ordered to turn and go back for a distance, probably to await the caravan in some ravine, and that they were now not very far away. It was necessary, then, to be as expeditious as possible.

He hastily returned and gave the order that the route of the caravan be changed, and that the party should cross over the hills and proceed by a route close to the Red Sea until the place of danger was left behind.

This was accordingly done, and the long lines passed anxiously yet laboriously onward over flinty summits, down steep and rugged hillsides, past rocky clefts and over barren desert spots peopled only by the echoes that rang from the mountain sides, until at last the sparkling waters of the Red Sea lay below, and the anxious travelers felt that, for the present at least, they were safe.

CHAPTER XIV.

THE BATTLE OF BEDR.

"A Prodigy of Fear, and a portent
Of broached mischief to the unborn times."
—Shakespeare.

The afternoon was intensely warm. Although the heat of the day was past, the houses of Mecca seemed to bake in the sun, the sand burned like a furnace, and a visible, shimmering heat seemed to fill the air. Nevertheless the ceremonies of Tawaf and the ablutions of Zem-Zem went on unceasingly, for it was the month of Ramadhan, and the half naked pilgrims, with their scanty white garments, shaven heads, and bare feet, kept up the perpetual promenade about the temple, even when so hot as to be ready to drop of exhaustion. The courtyard was crowded with people, the carriers of Zem-Zem water were in constant demand, and, in the cooler recesses of the covered portico around the great yard, a humming trade went on, the venders' cries rising above the prayers of the pilgrims.

Such was the scene upon which Omair suddenly staggered, all breathless, with haggard face, turban awry, and thin wisps of hair streaming in wet hanks over his brow.

"Where is Abu Jahl?" he cried, gasping.

"Why, what is wrong? Tell us!" cried the curious crowd in some consternation. "Where is Abu Sofian? Where is the caravan? Why have you come alone?"

"Send me Abu Jahl!" was his only reply.

The old man happened to be at the Caaba, and came anxiously at the unexpected summons.

"Omair!" he exclaimed. "Allah! What has happened?"

"Send them help!" gasped Omair. "Send them help at once, or not one in our fair caravan may escape! Mohammed is lying in wait for them in the mountain passes."

"May Allah have mercy!" ejaculated the old man; and the crowd about shrieked and groaned.

"Bring me the stair!" called Abu Jahl. "Place it close to the Caaba!"

This done, he ascended to the roof where all might see him. His snowy beard descended to his waist over his flowing garments, and his white locks fell thinly from beneath his kufiyah.

Silence fell upon the assembly below, and from every street men came hurrying in to hear the strange tidings.

"In the name of Allah, hear!" called Abu Jahl in loud tones. "Ye of the tribe of Koreish, hear! Ye who love Abu Sofian, hear! Ye who have friends or goods in the great caravan from Syria, hear! Ye above whom the arch-impostor, Mohammed, aspires, and whom he would fain crush beneath his feet as the vile serpent in the dust, hear! He hath beset our friends in the fastnesses of the mountains. He swoopeth upon them as the eagle upon the defenceless lamb out of the fold! Who, then, among you, will follow Abu Jahl to deliver them?"

An approving murmur rose, long and loud; then a hush fell as the aged man continued, appealing to the courage of his hearers:

"Ye who fear not the foul rebel's sword, ye who would uphold the honor of your wives and little ones, nor send your children out upon the world as the offspring of cowards, beseech your gods for blessing, then mount, and meet me as soon as may be outside the temple gates. In the name of Allah, good speed!"

A shout of assent arose. The thoroughly excited multitude swayed and surged like the waves of the sea. Hundreds hurried off to do the behest of their leader, and, returning, hastened to perform Tawaf about the Caaba before setting out on their perilous journey.

Yusuf, as a Christian, dared not enter the temple; but he heard the news from without. His heart was moved with compassion for the poor, defenceless traders, caught like mice in a trap, and he decided to fall into the ranks of the rescue party, intending, if his life were spared, to pay a visit to Amzi, at Medina.

While the recruits were gathering, Henda, the wife of Abu Sofian, rushed up, her face wild and haggard with terror, her long black hair streaming on the wind, her eyes flashing with excitement, and her lips drawn back, exposing her yellow, fanglike teeth. A tigress she looked in her fury, and it was with difficulty that Abu Jahl prevented her from going with the expedition, which, in the cooler shades of evening, started off at a rapid pace, leaving her to nurse her vengeance until a later day.

Hurried, yet long and tedious, was the journey, and the anxiety and impatience of the volunteers made it seem almost interminable.

At length news was brought of the safety of the caravan, and of its deviation towards the sea. But the blood of the Meccans was up, and the fiery old leader was determined to punish Mohammed for his misconduct, and thus, perhaps, prevent him from committing similar atrocities in the future. Accordingly he sent part of his troops for protection to the caravan, and commanded the rest, about nine hundred in number, to push on; and among those ordered forward to the field was Yusuf.

Mohammed, with three hundred and thirteen soldiers, mounted chiefly on camels, received word of this advance. His men were lying between Medina and the sea, and, as he thought, directly between the caravan and Abu Jahl's army. He told his men to be of good cheer, as Allah had promised them an easy victory; yet he was careful to omit no human means of securing an advantage. He posted his troops beside the brook Bedr, and had them hastily throw up an entrenchment to cover the flank of his troops. Then, sure of a constant supply of water, and safe from fear of surprise, he awaited the Meccan army.

He himself ascended a little eminence, accompanied only by Abu Beker, and, in a small hut made of branches, he prayed for the assistance of three thousand angels. In his excitement, one of his old paroxysms came on, but this was regarded as auspicious by his men, to whom, superstitious as they were, every occurrence of this kind was an additional presage of victory and an additional spur to bravery in battle.

And now the opposing force appeared, coming down the opposite hill, the men hot, weary, and covered with dust.

After a preliminary skirmish between individual combatants, the battle began,—not a systematic charge in close ranks, not the disciplined attack of trained warriors, but a wild mêlée of camels, horses, flashing scimitars, gleaming daggers and plunging spears, in the midst of clouds of dust and streaming scarfs.

The combat was long, and at one time the party of Mohammed seemed to waver. The prophet rushed out, threw a handful of dust into the air and exclaimed:

"May confusion light upon their faces! Charge, ye faithful! charge for Allah and his prophet!"

Nothing could withstand the wild dash made by his men. Filled with the passion of enthusiasm, the zeal of fanatics, and the confidence of success, they bore down like madmen. The Koreish, many of whom were fearful of enchantment by the prophet, were seized with sudden panic. In vain Abu Jahl tried to rally them. He was torn from his horse by a savage Moslem, and his head severed from his body. His troops fled in terror, leaving seventy men dead on the field and seventy prisoners.

The bodies and prisoners were robbed, and the spoil divided. Mohammed, in order to avert dispute over the booty, very conveniently had a revelation at the time.—"Know that whenever ye gain any spoil, a fifth part thereof belongeth unto God, and to the apostle, and to his kindred, and the orphans, and the poor, and the traveler."

Upon this occasion he claimed a considerable amount of silver, and a sword, Dhu'l Fakar (or the Piercer), which he carried in every subsequent battle.

During the battle, Yusuf, the priest, had fought bravely. Mounted on a magnificent horse, his commanding figure had marked him out as an object worthy of attack. Accordingly he was ever in the thickest of the fight. With cool and calm determination his blows fell, until suddenly an event occurred which completely unmanned him, and gave his enemies the advantage.

Among the opponents who singled him out for attack was a youth mounted on a horse of equal power and agility. The youth was rather slight, but his skill in thrusting and in averting strokes, and his evidence of practice in every exercise of the lance, rendered him a fitting adversary for the priest with his superior strength.

For some time their combat had gone on singlehanded, when the youth's headdress falling off revealed a face strikingly familiar to Yusuf. It was Manasseh's own face, pale, and with clots of blood upon it!

The priest was horrorstricken. He forbore to thrust, and the youth, seizing the opportunity, made a quick lunge, piercing the priest's shoulder, and felling him to the ground. A new opponent came and engaged the youth's attention; the panic fell, and the priest, seeing that it was useless to remain, managed to mount and ride off after the retreating troops.

Scarcely injured, yet covered with blood, he dismounted at Amzi's door in Medina.

"Yusuf! My brother!" cried the Meccan in astonishment, "what means this?"

In a few words Yusuf told the tale of the battle, and Amzi placed him comfortably upon a soft couch, insisting upon ministering to him as though he had been severely wounded.

"So, Yusuf the gentle too has become a seeker of man's blood!" he said. "Verily, what an effect hath this degenerate age!"

"Believe me, friend," returned the other, earnestly, "you too would have gone had you been in Mecca and had heard of our poor friends, all unarmed, and apparently in the power of the enemy. When the advance to Bedr was ordered, I was one under authority, and had no choice but to submit, though I had little enough love for the stench of blood."

"Yet," returned Amzi, "Yusuf's life is too precious to be risked in such madness. It is not necessary for him to court death; for the time may soon come when he shall be forced to fight in self defence. Till then, let foolish youths dash to the lance's point if they will."

Yusuf bowed his head, and in a low tone replied: "'O God, the Lord, the strength of my salvation, thou hast covered my head in the day of battle. He hath delivered my soul in peace from the battle that was against me. Yea, though I walk through the valley of the shadow of death, I will fear no evil, for thou art with me. He that dwelleth in the secret place of the Most High shall abide under the shadow of the Almighty. I will say of the Lord, He is my refuge and my fortress: my God; in him will I trust.' Amzi, whether in life or in death, it shall be as he wills."

Amzi looked at him curiously. "Yusuf," he said, "is there no extremity of your life in which your religion fails to give you comfort? It seems to furnish you with words befitting every occasion."

"Comfort in every hour of need," returned Yusuf, "deliverance in every hour of temptation, is our God able to bestow if we seek him in spirit and in truth. Things temporal, as well as things spiritual, call for his almighty love and attention; and our love for him brightens every pathway in life. It is the knowledge of this which has upheld his children in all the ages;—not one of them who has not gloried in feeling that 'God is our refuge and strength, a very present help in time of trouble. Therefore will we not fear, though the earth be removed, and though the mountains be carried into the midst of the sea.' Not one of them but has at some time found comfort in the promises, 'When the poor and the needy seek water, and there is none, and their tongue faileth for thirst, I the Lord will hear them; I, the God of Israel, will not forsake them. He that keepeth Israel slumbers not, nor sleeps. Fear thou not, for I am with thee; be not dismayed, for I am thy God; I will strengthen thee; yea, I will help thee; yea, I will uphold thee with the right hand of my righteousness.' Think of this help, Amzi, in every struggle: in the struggle, worse than any time of battle, with one's own sinful heart. And there is not one of God's children but has realized the blessedness of following the commands of Jesus, 'Have faith in God. Ask, and it shall be given you; seek, and ye shall find; knock, and it shall be opened unto you.' Amzi, you who love gentleness and peace, truth and humility, cannot you find in Christ and his loving precepts all you would ask? Can anything appeal to your warm heart more than such injunctions as these?—'Love your enemies, bless them that curse you, do good to them that hate you, and pray for them that despitefully use you and persecute you. When thou doest alms, let not thy left hand know what thy right hand doeth. Let your light so shine before men, that they may see your good works, and glorify your Father which is in heaven. Judge not, that ye be not judged. Watch ye, therefore, and pray always. Pray that ye enter not into temptation.'"

He paused, out of breath; for such had been his study of the Scriptures that the words came in a flood to his lips.

Amzi sighed. "Yes, Yusuf," he said, "such words seem to me full of goodness and sweetness; yet, try as I may, I cannot realize their true import. I cannot rejoice, as you and your friends do, in your religion and its promises."

"My Amzi," returned the priest, "how can you be warmed except you come to the fire? Remember the man with the withered hand. Did he not stretch it out in faith? My friend, like him, act! Reach out your heart to God. He will not fail you. Look not upon yourself. Look upon God, who is, indeed, closer to you than you can imagine. Put your hand in his, behold his love manifested to us in the coming of his dear Son, and feel that that love is today the same, proceeding from the Father in whom is 'no variableness, neither shadow of turning.'"

Amzi sighed. "Yusuf," he said, "it appears all dark, impenetrable, to me. A wall of adamant seems to stand between me and God. Pray for me, friend. In this matter I fear I am heartless."

In spite of this assertion, there was genuine concern in the tone, and the priest's face flushed in the glad light of hope.

"Amzi," he exclaimed, "my hope for you increases. Even now, you begin to realize your own self: it remains for you to realize God's self. Know God—would I could burn that upon your heart! All else would be made plain."

Amzi sighed again. For a time he sat in silence, then he said:

"I have been reading of the tabernacle, and of the sacrifices therein."

"Typical of the death of Christ," returned Yusuf. "A constant emblem of that mind which was, and is today, ready to suffer, that we may understand its infinite love."

"Strange, strange!" said Amzi, musingly. Then after a long silence: "Yusuf, have you ever noted the resemblance of the Caaba to the reputed appearance of the tabernacle?"

"The resemblance struck me from the first glance—the courtyard, the temple itself, and the curtain (or 'Kiswah') corresponding to the veil of the tabernacle. This same Caaba may trace its origin in some dim way to the ancient tabernacle, of which, in this land, the significance must have become lost in the centuries during which the Ishmaelitish race forgot the true worship of God."

"And what think you of the course which affairs are now taking in Arabia?" asked Amzi. "You believe in the supervision of God; why, then, does he permit such outbreaks as the present one is proving to be?"

"I certainly believe that the Creator sees and knows all things. I believe, too, that even to Mohammed, at one time in his life, the Holy Spirit appealed, as he did to me, and, I hope, does now to you, Amzi,—for his pleadings come sometime to all men; but, I think that if in earnest at first, Mohammed—if, indeed, he be not a monomaniac on the subject of his divine calling—has given himself up to the wild indulgence of his ambition, forgetting Him whose power is able to direct us all aright. Hence, he guides himself, rather than seeks to be guided, and, in such a case, he may sometimes be allowed to go on in his own way, bearing with him those who are so foolish as to accept his teaching. Something of this kind may, indeed, be one of the secrets of the crimes and calamities which enter into many human lives. God leaves us free to choose. When we come to know him we choose to be his followers. If we are indifferent to him, he may, at times, look on without interfering in our lives except to send us occasionally great trouble, or great joy, as an appeal to us. His mercy is great. He pities and pleads with us, yet he leaves us free."

"And what, think you, will be the effect upon Arabia of this rising?"

Yusuf shook his head. "I know not," he said. "We cannot see now, nor mayhap until ages have rolled by; but 'at eventide it shall be light.'"

So talked Amzi and the priest until the gray dawn shone in, and the voice of Bilal, the muezzin, was heard calling from the mosque:

"God is great! There is no God but God! Mohammed is the prophet of God! Come to prayers! God is great!"

CHAPTER XV.

THE PERSECUTION BEGINS.

*"In doing good we are generally cold and languid and slug-
gish . . . . But the works of Malice and Injustice are quite in
another style."*
—Burke.

Among those left dead on the field of Bedr were the father,
uncle and brother of Henda, the wife of Abu Sofian. Fierce and
savage as was her nature, she was yet capable of deep feeling, and
her love for her kindred was one of the ruling passions of her life.

When the caravan at last reached Mecca in safety, she rushed
to meet Abu Sofian, weeping wildly, wringing her hands in grief,
and throwing dust on her long hair. She besought him frantically
to avenge their death, and he, knowing that the debt of "blood
revenge" was now upon him, and that blood alone would wipe the
stain from his honor, gathered two hundred swift horsemen and
set out almost immediately for Medina.

On the way he ravaged the whole country, burning the villages
and date groves of Mohammed's followers.

When within three miles of Medina the prophet sallied out to
meet him. A brief contest took place, and Abu Sofian was once
more defeated in what was jestingly called the Battle of the Meal
Sacks.

The Moslems were exultant over their success, but Abu Sofian
returned to Mecca, the blood-dues still unpaid, and with bitter
enmity gnawing at his heart.

In the meantime Mohammed began to assume all the airs of
an independent sovereign. He married a beautiful maiden, Hafza,
to whom he entrusted the care of the Koran, according as it was
revealed; and shortly afterwards he issued a decree by which all
true believers were ordered to face Mecca when praying. Thus
early in his career of conquest he had fixed upon Mecca as the
future holy city of the Moslems. As usual, the Koran was called in
to authorize him in thus fixing the Kebla, or point of prayer.

"Unto God belongeth the East and the West. He directeth
whom he pleaseth in the right way. Turn, therefore, thy face
towards the holy temple of Mecca; and wherever ye be, turn your
faces towards that place."

At this time also he sanctioned the retaining of the holy fast of

Ramadhan and the pilgrimages connected therewith. As he was well aware that the doing away with the great bazar upon which the prosperity of Mecca so largely depended would loose a host of enemies upon him, he declared:

"O true believers, a fast is ordained you, as it was ordained unto them before you, that ye may fear God. The month of Ramadhan shall ye fast, in which the Koran was sent down from heaven, a direction unto men."

Henceforth, during the fast, all true believers were to abstain from eating or drinking, and from all earthly pleasures, while the sun shone above the horizon and until the lamps at the mosques were lighted by the Imaums. It is needless to say that the Moslems obviated this self sacrifice by sleeping during the day as much as possible, giving the night up to all the proscribed indulgences of the interdicted season.

And now Mohammed's hatred to the Jews began to show itself, and the awful persecution of the little Jewish band in Medina commenced.

Poor Dumah was one of the first to bring the rod of wrath upon himself. When wandering down the street one day, not very long after the Battle of Bedr, he paused by a well, just as Mohammed, accompanied by his faithful Zeid, appeared in the way. Dumah saw them and at once began to sing his thoughts in a wild, irregular lament. His voice was peculiarly sweet and clear, and every word reached the ear of the enraged prophet. The song was a weird lament over those slain at Bedr:

> *"They are fallen, the good are fallen,*
> *Low in the dust they are fallen;*
> *And their hair is steeped in blood;*
> *But the poison-wind shrieks above them,*
> *Sighing anon like the cushat,*
> *And breathing its curses upon him,*
> *Upon him, the chief of impostors.*
> *As he passes the leaflets tremble,*
> *And the flowers shrink from his pathway;*
> *And the angels smile not upon him,*
> *For he maketh the widow and orphan;*
> *And the voice of Rachel riseth*
> *In mourning loud for her children.*
> *And no comfort doth fall upon her.*
> *Soft like the balm of Gilead."*

Turning to one of his followers, Mohammed commanded angrily:

"Seize that singer!"

Dumah heard the exclamation, and was off like the wind, followed by two or three Moslems, each anxious to secure the victim first, and thus win the approval of the august Mohammed.

On, on, straight to the house of Amzi fled Dumah. Bursting open the door, he rushed in, his long hair disordered, his face purple with running and his eyes wide with terror.

"Save me, Yusuf! Save me, Amzi!" he cried. "Mohammed will kill me! Mohammed will kill me!"

Yusuf sprang to the door, and the poor fugitive threw himself at Amzi's feet, clinging to his garments with his thin, white hands.

But the pursuers were already upon him. Yusuf strove in vain to detain them, to reason with them.

"Can you not see he is a poor artless lad? Can you not have mercy?" he cried.

"It is the order of the prophet of Allah!" was the response.

Yusuf resisted their entrance with all his might, but, unarmed as he was, he was quickly thrown down, and the terrified Dumah was dragged over his body and hurried off to be put in chains in a Moslem cell.

Amzi was distracted. There seemed little hope for Dumah. The small Jewish band then in Medina could not dare to cope with the overwhelming numbers of Moslems that swarmed in the streets. If Dumah were delivered it must be by stratagem; and yet what stratagem could be employed?

Early in the evening Amzi and the priest withdrew to the roof for consultation.

"You believe that your God is all-powerful—why do you not beseech him for our poor lad's safety?" cried Amzi passionately.

"I have not ceased to do so since his capture," returned Yusuf. "But it must be as the Lord willeth. He sees what is best. Even our blessed Jesus said to the Father, 'Not my will, but thine be done.'"

Amzi was not satisfied. "Can he then be the God of Love that you say, if he could look upon the death of that poor innocent nor exercise his power to save him?"

"Amzi, I do not wonder at you for speaking thus. Yet consider. We will hope the best for our poor singer. May God preserve him and enable us, as instruments in his hands, to deliver him. But God may see differently from us in this matter. Who can say that to die would not be gain to poor Dumah? All witless as he is, he shall have a perfect mind and a perfect body in the bright hereafter. We know not what is well. We can only pray and do all in our power to effect his deliverance; we must leave the issue to God."

Amzi bowed his head on his hands and groaned. Yusuf raised his eyes towards heaven; the tears rolled down his cheeks, and his lips moved. Even he could not understand the mysteries of this strange time. Yet he was constantly comforted in knowing that "all things work together for good to them that love God."

Saddest of all was the vision of the handsome, dark face that, contorted in the fury of combat, had glared upon him from the Moslem ranks in the Battle of Bedr, while Manasseh's hand showered blows upon the head of his best friend—for the sake of the prophet of Islam.

"Manasseh! Manasseh!" he exclaimed in bitter sadness. "Why hast thou forsaken thy father's God? O heavenly Father, do thou guide him and lead him again into thy paths!"

CHAPTER XVI.

AMZI FINALLY REJECTS MOHAMMED.

"'Do the duty which lies nearest thee' which thou knowest to be a duty! Thy second duty will already have become clearer."
—Carlyle, "Sartor Resartus."

Upon the following morning Yusuf hastened to obtain an interview with Mohammed. The prophet lived in an ostentatiously humble abode—a low, broad building, roofed with datesticks, and thatched with the broad leaves of the palm tree.

Mohammed absolutely refused to see him. Ayesha, the youngest and fairest of the prophet's wives, sent to inform him that Mohammed had nothing to say to the Christian Yusuf. So with heavy heart he turned away and sought the house of Zeid, deeming that he, as the prophet's adopted son and most devoted follower, might have some influence in obtaining Dumah's release.

Zeid sat in a low, airy apartment, through whose many open windows a cool breeze entered. By him sat his newly wedded wife, unveiled, for at that time the rules in regard to veiling were not so strictly insisted upon as at a later day, when the prophet's decree against the unveiling of women was more rigorously enforced.

Even Yusuf noted her marvelous beauty. There was a peculiarity of action, a something familiar about her, too, which gave him a hazy recollection of having seen her before; but not for several moments did the association come up in his memory, and he saw again the little Jewish home of Nathan in Mecca, the dim light, and the beautiful child whose temples Nathan's wife was so tenderly bathing. Yes, after the lapse of years, in a flash he knew her for Zeinab!

She listened with interest to the tale of the Jewish singer; but there was a heartlessness in her air, and a certain contempt in the look which she bent upon the Christian who was thus making intercession for an unworthy Jew.

"I have neither eyes to see, tongue to speak, nor hands to act, save as the prophet is pleased to direct me," was Zeid's reply, in the most determined tone.

Yusuf, seeing no hope, left the house, and shortly afterwards Zeid, too, went down into the town. Scarcely had he left when

Mohammed entered.

Zeinab was still at the window, which opened directly on the courtyard. A myrtle bush grew near, and she listlessly plucked some of the white blossoms and twined them in the braids of her glossy black hair. She wore a loose gown of sky-blue silk with a drape of crimson, and deep pointed sleeves of filmy, white lace. Her veil was cast aside, and when the prophet entered she turned her magnificent dark eyes, with their shading of kohl, full upon him.

Ever susceptible to the influence of beauty, he exclaimed, "Praise be God, who turneth the hearts of men as he pleaseth!" And he at once coveted her for his wife; although according to law she bore the relation of daughter to him.

He intimated his desire to Ali, who, in turn, broke the news to Zeid. Zeid returned pale and trembling to his home. He loved his wife deeply; yet his devotion to the prophet and the sense of obligation which he owed him as foster-father, for having freed him from servitude, appealed to him strongly. Bowing his head upon his wife's knee, he wept.

"Why do you weep, Zeid?" she asked.

"Alas!" he cried, "could one who has known thee as wife forbear to weep at having thee leave him?"

"But I will never leave my Zeid."

"Not even to become the wife of the prophet?"

"Mohammed does not want me for his wife," she said quickly.

Zeid sighed. "Could you be happy were you his wife?" he asked.

The beauty's ambitious spirit rose, but she only said: "Were I made his wife, it would be the will of Allah."

Zeid pushed her gently from him, and went out. "Mohammed," he said, seating himself at the prophet's feet, "you care for Zeinab. I come to offer her to you. Obtain for your poor Zeid a writ of divorce."

The prophet's face showed his satisfaction. "I could never accept such a sacrifice," he said, hesitatingly.

"My life, my all, even to my beloved wife, belongs to my master," returned Zeid. "His pleasure stands to me before aught else."

"So be it, then, most faithful," said the prophet. "O Zeid, my more than son, a glorious reward is withheld for you."

Then, as ever, a revelation of the Koran came seasonably ere another day, to remove every impediment to the union of Mohammed and Zeinab.

"But when Zeid had determined the matter concerning her, and had resolved to divorce her, we joined her in marriage unto thee, lest a crime should be charged on the true believers in marrying the wives of their adopted sons: and the command of God is to be performed. No crime is to be charged on the prophet as to what God hath allowed him."

There were those in Medina who resented Mohammed's selfishness in thus appropriating Zeinab to himself, and there were those who questioned the honor of such a proceeding; but this questioning went on mostly among the few Bedouin adherents who had flocked into the town in his service, for the most sacred oath of the highest class of Bedouins has long been, "By the honor of my women!"

In none did the prophet's action inspire more disgust than in our two friends, Yusuf and Amzi. Amzi had long since lost all faith in the prophet as a divine representative; and this marriage with Zeinab only confirmed his distrust.

"Pah!" he said to Yusuf, "he not only lets his own impulses sway him, but he uses the sanction of heaven to authorize the satisfaction of every desire, no matter who is trampled upon in the proceeding. Was there ever such sacrilege?"

Yusuf returned: "For this I am thankful, brother: that you at last apply the term 'sacrilege' to the claims of this impostor."

"Think you he is no longer in earnest at all for the raising of his countrymen from idolatry?"

"He seeks to throw down idols, but to raise himself in their stead. Cupidity and ambition, Amzi, have well-nigh smothered every struggling seed of good in Mohammed's haughty bosom."

"Do you not think that, at the beginning, he imagined himself inspired?"

"Mohammed is strangely visionary. At the beginning he, doubtless, thought he saw visions, but, if the man thinks himself inspired now, he is mad."

"Yet what a personality he has!" said Amzi, musingly. "What a charm he bears! How his least word is sufficient to move this crowd of howling fanatics!"

"A man who might be an angel of light, were he truly under divine guidance," returned Yusuf. "And, mark me, Amzi, his influence will not stop with this generation. The influence of every man on God's earth goes on ever-rolling, ever-unceasing, down the long tide of eternity; but, in every age, there are those who, like Mohammed, possess such an individuality, such a personality, that their power goes on increasing, crashing like the avalanche down my native mountains."

"How eloquently such a thought appeals to right impulse, right action!" said Amzi, thoughtfully. "Did a man realize its import fully, he would surely be spurred on to act, not to sit idly letting the world drift by."

"'No man liveth unto himself,'" said Yusuf slowly. "Whether we will it or not, we are each of us ever exerting some influence for good or for ill upon those with whom we come in contact. No one can be neutral. Acts often speak in thunder-tones, when mere words are heard but in whispers."

"I fear me, Yusuf," said the Meccan, with a half smile, "that Amzi has neither thundered in action, nor even whispered in words. So little good has he done, that he almost hates to think of your great influence theory."

Yusuf smiled and slipped his arm about the Meccan's shoulder. "Amzi, the name of 'benevolent' belies your words," he said. "Think you that your home duties faithfully performed, your pure and upright life, pass for naught?"

"You would stand aghast, Yusuf," returned Amzi, "if I told you the amount of time that I have squandered, simply in dreaming, smoking, and taking my ease."

"Time is a precious gift," replied Yusuf, "it flows on and on as a great river towards the sea, and never returns. It appears to me, every day, more clearly as the talent given to all men to be used rightly. I, as well as you, have let precious hours pass, and, in doing so, we have both done wrong. Yet I pray that we may every day see, more and more, the necessity of well occupying the hours,—'redeeming the time, because the days are evil.'"

"Would that I had your decision of purpose, your firmness of will!" said Amzi, wistfully. "Yusuf, it would be impossible for me to spend all my time as you do,—visiting, relieving, studying, speaking ever the word in season, and ever working for others. I should miss my *kaif*."

"Even if you know it was in the cause of the Lord?" asked Yusuf, with gentle reproof. "Yet, Amzi, you have done as much as I, considering your opportunities. The great thing is to do faithfully whatever comes to one's hand, whether that be great or small. Know you not that it was said to him who had received only two talents, 'Well done, good and faithful servant; thou hast been faithful over a few things, I will make thee ruler over many things.' As bright crowns await the humble home-workers as the great movers of earth, provided all be done 'as unto the Lord.'"

"But," returned Amzi, impatiently, "my 'good works,' as you

call them, have not been done 'as unto the Lord.' My charities have been done simply because the sight of misery caused me to feel unhappy. I felt pity for the wretched, and in relieving them set my own mind at ease, and gave satisfaction to myself. I feel that it is right to do certain things, and so I do them under a sense of moral obligation."

"Then," said Yusuf, "has this acting under a sense of moral obligation brought you perfect satisfaction, perfect rest?"

"Frankly, it has not."

Yusuf rose, and, placing both hands on Amzi's shoulders, said earnestly: "My friend, who can say that every good impulse of man may not be an outcome of the divine nature implanted in him by the Creator, and which, if watered and developed, will surely burst into the flower of goodness when once the influence of God's Spirit is fully recognized and ever invoked? Amzi, you have many such seeds of innate good. Your very longings for good, your tone of late, show me that you are near this blessed recognition. Why will you not believe? Why will you not embrace the Lord Jesus Christ? We are all weak of ourselves, but we have strength in him. Amzi, my friend, pray for yourself."

He turned abruptly and left Amzi alone, to ponder long and earnestly over the conversation of the past hour.

CHAPTER XVII.

THE FATE OF DUMAH.

*"Death is the liberator of him whom freedom cannot release,
the physician of him whom medicine cannot cure, and the
comforter of him whom time cannot console."*
—Colton.

And now began a veritable reign of terror for the Jews of
Medina. The first evidence of the closing of Mohammed's iron
hand was shown in his forcing them to make Mecca, rather than
Jerusalem, their kebla, or point of prayer. Many refused to obey
this command, and were consequently dragged off to await the
pleasure of the prophet.

At first the keenest edge of Moslem vindictiveness seemed to
be directed against the bards or poets, for the power of stirring
and pathetic poetry in arousing the passionate Oriental blood to
revenge was recognized as an instrument too potent to be over-
looked.

Ere long even the form of imprisonment was, to a great extent,
set aside, and the knife of the assassin was set at work. Among
those who thus fell were Kaab, a Jewish poet who strove to incite
the Koreish to aggressive measures against the Moslems; and
Assina, a young woman who had been guilty of writing satires
directed against the prophet himself.

Yusuf and Amzi became greatly alarmed for the safety of
Dumah. Every possible means of rendering assistance to the poor
singer seemed to be cut off. They could not even find any clue to
his whereabouts, and feared that he, too, had fallen beneath some
treacherous blade.

As yet, Amzi and Yusuf had been permitted to wander at will.
For hours and hours did they roam about the streets seeking for
some clue to Dumah's place of imprisonment, but all efforts were
futile, until one day Amzi heard a faint voice singing in the cellar
of one of the Moslem buildings. He lay down by the wall, closed
his eyes, and strained his ears to catch the sound. It was assuredly
Dumah, singing weakly:

> *"Oh, why will they not come,*
> *The friends of Dumah!*
> *For living death is upon him,*

And the walls of his tomb close over,
Yet will not in mercy fall on him.
Does the sun shine still on the mountain,
And the trees wave?
Do the birds still sing in the palm trees,
And the flowers still bloom in Kuba?
And yet doth Dumah languish

"But Dumah's friends have forgotten him,
Nor seek him more,
And even the angels vanish,
And the tomb is all about him:
O Death, come, haste to Dumah!"

The voice sank away in a low wail, and Amzi sprang up. His first impulse was to rush in and batter at the door of Dumah's cell; his second, to call words of comfort through the wall. Yet either would be imprudent and might ruin all, so he hastened home to Yusuf.

"I will go to him immediately," said the priest.

"But how?"

"In disguise if need be," was the reply.

"In disguise!" exclaimed Amzi. "Friend, with your physique, think you you can disguise yourself? Not a Moslem in Mecca who does not know the figure of Yusuf the Christian. Nay, Yusuf, your friend Amzi can effect a disguise much more easily. Here,"—running his fingers through his gray beard,—"a few grains of black dye can soon transform this; some stain will change the Meccan's ruddy cheeks into the brown of a desert Arab. The thing is easy."

"As you will, then," said the priest; and the two were soon busy at work at the transforming process.

With the garb of a Moslem soldier, Amzi was soon, to all appearance, a passable Mussulman, with divided beard, and chocolate-brown skin.

He set out, and, having arrived at the door of the sort of barracks in which Dumah was imprisoned, mingled with the soldiers, quite unnoticed among the new arrivals who constantly swelled the prophet's army.

With the greatest difficulty, yet without exciting apparent suspicion, he found out the exact spot in which Dumah was confined. Upon the first opportunity he slipped noiselessly after the attendant who was carrying the prisoner's pittance of food. Under his robe he had tools for excavating a hole beneath the wall, and his plan was to step silently into the room, secrete himself behind the door, and permit himself to be locked in, trusting to subsequent efforts for effecting the freedom of himself and Dumah.

Silently he glided into the darkened room behind the keeper. All within seemed dark as night after the brighter light without; but Dumah's eyes, accustomed to the darkness, could see more clearly. He penetrated the disguise at once.

"Amzi! Amzi!" he cried out delightedly, "you have come! You have come!"

Amzi knew that all was undone.

"Treachery!" called the keeper.

The Moslems came pouring into the room. Amzi was over-powered, and pinioned on the spot.

"What means this?" cried Asru, the captain of the guard.

"Treachery, if it please you," returned the keeper. "An asp which has been in our camp with its poison-fangs hid! No Moslem, but an enemy—a friend of this dotard poet!"

"Search him!" was the order.

The tools were found.

"Aha!" said the captain. "Most conclusive proof, wretch! We will teach you, knave, that foxes are sometimes trapped in their own wiles. Off with him! Chain him!"

Amzi was hurried off, and Asru strode away to execute some other act of so-called justice. He was a man of immense stature, heavy featured, and covered with pockmarks, yet his face was full of strength of character, and bore traces of candor and honesty, though the lines about the mouth told of unrestrained cruelty and passion.

At home Yusuf waited in an agony of suspense. The day passed into night, the night into day, the day into night again, yet Amzi did not come. Yusuf could bear it no longer. Anything was better than this awful waiting. Only once he almost gave up hope and cried in the words of the Psalmist, "O Lord, why castest thou off my soul? Why hidest thou thy face from me?" Then like balm of healing came the words, "Cast thy burden upon the Lord, and he will sustain thee; he shall never suffer the righteous to be moved."

Dressed in his quiet, scholarly raiment, and quite unarmed, he set out in search of Amzi. Arriving at the place, he saw none whom he knew. He was stopped at the door.

"I wish to see the captain who has command here," he said.

"You are a peaceable looking citizen enough," said a guard, "yet we have orders to search all newcomers, and you will have to submit, stranger."

Yusuf was searched, but as neither arms nor tools were found upon him, he was allowed to have audience with the captain.

"Ah!" said Asru, recognizing him at once. "What seeks Yusuf, a Christian, of a follower of Mohammed the prophet?"

"I seek but the deliverance of two harmless, inoffensive friends," he replied.

"A bold request, truly," said the other. "Yet have I not forgotten my debt of gratitude to you. I have not forgotten that it was Yusuf who nursed me through the foul disease whose marks I yet bear, when all others fled;" and he passed his hand over his pock-marked face.

"Of that speak not," returned Yusuf, with a gesture of impatience. "'Twas but the service which any man with a heart may render to a needy brother. However, if you are grateful, as you say, you can more than repay the debt, you can make me indebted to you, by telling me aught of Amzi, the benevolent Meccan, whose hand would not take the life of a worm were he not forced into it."

"He is here in chains," said Asru haughtily, "as every spy who enters a Moslem camp should be."

"Amzi is no spy!" declared Yusuf emphatically.

"His sole object, then, was to free that half-witted poet?" asked Asru, incredulously.

"It was none other. He loves him as his own son, as do I. Amzi would suffer death willingly, Yusuf would suffer death willingly, would it spare that poor, confiding innocent!"

The priest's eyes were flashing, and his tones bore witness to his earnestness. He did not notice, nor did Asru, a pair of bright eyes that peered at him from the chink of the doorway; he did not know that a face full of petty, vindictive spite was partially hidden by the darkness without, or that two keen ears were listening to every word he said.

"Yusuf," returned the captain in a low tone, "you are the only man who has ever seemed to me good. Your words, at least, are ever truth. You wonder, then, that I follow the prophet? Simply because the excitement of war suits me, and"—he shrugged his shoulders with a laugh—"it is the best policy to be on the winning side. Most of these crazed idiots believe in him, and fear that he will work enchantments upon them if they do not; but the doctrine of the sword and of plunder goes farther with a few, of whom Asru is one. Because I believe in you, Yusuf, I shall try to carry out your request. But it would cost me my life were it found out, so it must be seemingly by chance. Rest assured that, bad as I am, cruel as I am, I shall see that Yusuf's friends have some 'accidental' way of escape."

So spoke Asru, nor knew that a pair of feet were hurrying and shuffling towards the prophet, while a soldier kept guard at the door.

"May heaven bless you for this!" cried the priest. "So long as Amzi and Yusuf breathe you shall not lack an earthly friend."

"Tush!" exclaimed the captain. "'Tis but the wish to make old scores even. You serve me; I serve you. We are even."

"Then I shall leave you," said Yusuf, rising with a smile.

Asru opened the door.

"Hold!" cried a guard. "By order of the prophet, Asru is my prisoner!"

"Wherefore?" cried Asru, attempting to seize his dagger.

"Because, though it is politic to be on the winning side, it is not always safe to be a traitor and to countermand Mohammed's orders," replied the prophet's musical voice, as the soldiers gave way to permit his advance.

Asru freed himself and dashed forward, wielding his dagger right and left, but it was a rash effort. He was instantly overpowered and bound hand and foot. The priest shared the same fate.

The prophet looked down upon the captain. "Asru," he said, "you whom I deemed a most faithful one, you who have proved false, know that death is the meed of a traitor. Yet that you may know Mohammed can show mercy, I give you your life. For the sake of your past services I grant it you, and trust that, having learned obedience and humility, you may once again grace our battlefields nobly. Guards, chain him, yet see that he is kept in easy confinement and lacks nothing. Send me Uzza."

The Oman Arab came forward. He was a dark-browed man, undersized, and with one shoulder higher than the other. His eyes were long and narrow, with a look of extreme cunning about them, and his mouth was cruel, his lips being pressed together so tightly that they looked like a long white line.

"Upon you, Uzza, O faithful, as next in command, I confer the honor of the position left vacant by Asru. Do thou carry out its obligations with honor to thyself and to the prophet of Allah."

Uzza prostrated himself to the ground.

Mohammed turned to Yusuf. "Whom have we here? What said you in your accusation, Abraham? An accomplice of Asru, was it?"

The little peddler, the silent watcher at the door, came forward, hopping along as usual, but with malignant triumph in his face.

"This, O prophet," he said, making obeisance, "is not only an accomplice of Asru, but a sworn enemy of the prophet of Allah and of all who believe in him."

"Why, methinks I have seen him before," said Mohammed, passing his hand over his brow. "Is not this the gentle friend of Amzi?"

"He is the friend of Amzi," returned the Jew, "but even Amzi lies in chains as a spy among the Moslems."

"I had forgotten," said the prophet. "Yet what harm hath this gentle Meccan done?"

"He is Yusuf, the Magian priest," said the Jew. "And believe, O prophet of Allah, the Magians are your most bitter enemies."

Uzza started and leaned forward with intense interest. Yusuf felt his burning gaze fixed on his face.

"What proof have you that this is a Magian priest?" asked the prophet, wearily.

"See!" exclaimed the Jew.

He tore back the priest's garment, and there was the red mark of the torch outlined distinctly against the white skin.

"Ha!" cried Uzza, starting forward, the veins of his forehead swelling with excitement. "The very mark! The secret mark of the priests among those who worship fire and the sun! This, O Mohammed, is not only a priest, but a priest who has fed the temple fires, and as such has been pledged to uphold the Guebre religion at whatever cost."

Yusuf said nothing.

"Can you not speak, Yusuf?" asked Mohammed. "Have you no word to say to all this?"

"It is all true, O Mohammed," replied Yusuf, quietly. "It is true that in my youthful days I was a priest at Guebre altars. Now, I am not Yusuf the Magian priest, but Yusuf the Christian, and a humble follower of our Most High God and his Son Jesus."

"Dare you thus proclaim yourself a Christian to my very face?" exclaimed Mohammed. "Magian or Christian, ye are all alike enemies. Off with him! Do with him as you will, Uzza,—yet," relenting, "I commend him to your mercy." He turned abruptly and left the apartment.

Yusuf was immediately taken and thrown into a close, dark room. He was still bound hand and foot.

The little Jew entered, and sat down with his head on one side.

"Now, proud Yusuf," he said, "has come Abraham's day. Once it was Yusuf's day; then the poor peddler, the little dervish, was scourged and chained, and well-nigh smothered in that vile Meccan chamber. Now it has come Abraham's day, and Yusuf and Abraham will be even. How does this suit your angelic constitution? Angelic as you are, you cannot slip through chains and bolted doors so easily as the little Jew. Oh, Yusuf, are you not happy? Uzza hates you; I saw it in his face. Did you ever know him before?" The Jew's propensity for news was to the fore as usual.

Yusuf answered nothing.

"Tell me," said the Jew, giving him a shake, "what does Uzza know of you?"

"He knows," said a thin, grating voice from behind, "that Yusuf's hands reek with the blood of Uzza's only child, the fair little Imri, murdered in the cause of religion; and ere I could reach him—yes, priest, with vengeance in my heart, for had I found you then your blood would have blotted out the stain of my child's on your altar!—the false priest had fled, forsaken the reeking altar, left it black in ashes, black as his own false heart. And then, that vengeance might be satisfied, was Uzza's blade turned against the aged grandmother who had delivered the little one up to Persian gods. O priest, your work is past, but not forgotten!"

"Uzza," cried the priest, "I neither ask nor hope for mercy. Yet would God I could restore you your child! Its smile and its death gurgle have haunted my dreams through these long years! 'Twas in my heathendom I did it!"

"That excuse will not give her back to me," said Uzza, stepping out of the room with the Jew, as the warden came with the keys.

It was not Uzza's purpose to bring about Yusuf's speedy death. As the cat torments the mouse which has fallen into its power, so he resolved to keep the priest on the rack for a considerable length of time.

Hearing of the conversation between him and Asru, he knew that exquisite torture could be inflicted on the priest through Dumah, and determined to strike at him first through the poor singer. Dumah's execution was, accordingly, ordered.

Early one morning, Amzi, looking out of a little chink in his window through which the bare courtyard below was visible, was horrified to see a scene revolting in its every detail, and over which we shall hasten as speedily as may be.

There in the gray morning light stood Yusuf, bound and forced to look on at the death of the bright-haired singer, whose sunny smile had been as a ray of sunshine to the two men.

Amzi looked on as if turned to stone—heard Dumah's last

cheerful words, "Do not weep, Yusuf; it will be all flowers, all angels, soon. Dumah is going home happy,"—then, he fell on his face, and so lay for hours unconscious of all. Reason came slowly back, and he realized that another of the tragedies only too common in those perilous days had taken place.

"I am going home happy," rang in his ears. The cold moonlight crept in, shining in a dead silver bar on the ceiling. Amzi lay looking at it, until it seemed a path of glory leading, for Dumah's feet, through the window and up to heaven.

"I am going home happy." Was that home Amzi's home too? Ah, he had never thought of it as his home, though he remembered the words—"In my Father's house are many mansions." He imagined he saw Dumah in one of those bright mansions, happy in eternal love and sunshine, while he, Amzi, was without.

For the first time in his life Amzi was concerned deeply about his soul; and now there was no Yusuf to answer his questions. Ere another day had passed he, too, might be called upon to undergo Dumah's fate. He could not say "I am going home happy." How, then, might this blessed assurance be his? He strove to remember Yusuf's words, but they seemed to flit away from his memory. His whole life appeared so listless, so selfish, so taken up with gratification of self! At last he seemed a sinner. How could he obtain forgiveness?

He turned over in agony, and the little stone tablet fell against his bosom. With difficulty, on account of the manacles on his hands, he drew it forth and traced the words with his finger.

"For God so loved the world, that he gave his only begotten Son, that whosoever believeth in him should not perish, but have everlasting life."

As when a black cloud passes away from the moon and a flood of brightness fills the whole air below, so the light burst upon Amzi. He saw it all now! His talk with Yusuf on the love of God came back to him, and he shouted aloud with joy:

"Praise the Lord, he hath set me free!"

"Then for the sake of mercy, help me to get out of this too," said a voice from the other side of the partition. It was Asru.

"Alas, my friend," returned Amzi, "chains are still on my body. It is my soul that soareth upward as an eagle."

"Wherefore?"

Amzi read the verse of Scripture aloud.

"I have heard somewhat of that before," said Asru. "Read it again."

Amzi did so, and explained it as well as he could. Asru listened eagerly. This new creed interested him by its novelty, especially since he was in forced inaction and had nothing else to think of. But it also appealed to a heart which had some noble traits among many evil ones; and as Amzi talked, sorrow for his sins came upon him.

"But the promise cannot be given to such as I," he said, wistfully. "A long life of wickedness surely cannot win forgiveness."

"O friend," returned Amzi, eagerly, "'believe on the Lord Jesus Christ, and thou shalt be saved.' How often did they tell me those words and I would not believe, could not understand!"

And then Amzi told the story of the thief on the cross, as he had read it and talked it over with Yusuf. His voice thrilled with eagerness, and, on the other side of the wall, Asru wept tears of repentance. To him too, the door was opening, and a great longing for the love of Christ and for a better life filled his bosom. So they talked until the noise of the awakening Moslems in the passage without rendered it impossible for them to hear each other. But joy had come to both Amzi and Asru within the prison walls.

CHAPTER XVIII.

A SCENE IN PALESTINE.

"I had rather choose to be a pilgrim on earth with Thee than without Thee to possess heaven. Where Thou art, there is heaven: and where thou art not, there is death and hell."
—Thomas á Kempis.

It was a scene perfect in its calm beauty. A small, low, white house, flat roofed, and dazzlingly clean, nestled at the foot of one of the fairest hills in Palestine; and before the door swept the river Jordan, plashing with that low, soft ripple which is music everywhere, but nowhere more so than in the hot countries of the East.

A grove of banana and orange trees sheltered the house, and the delicate fragrance of the ripening fruit mingled with the perfume of late roses. On the green hills near, sheep rambled at will, and an occasional low bleat arose above the busy hum of bees, giving an air of life to the quiet scene.

In the shade of the trees sat Nathan, his wife and Mary. They had been talking of Manasseh,—poor Manasseh, left behind in barren Arabia! Nathan too had wanted to stay with his distressed countrymen, but failing health had forced him to seek the more genial atmosphere of the North; and, after a long, tedious journey, he at last found himself safe once more in his beloved Palestine, poor in worldly goods, yet serene and hopeful as ever.

And fortune was at last smiling on the Jewish family. Nathan's health had come back to him in the clearer, more bracing air of the Northern land, his flocks were increasing, and the only gloom upon their perfect happiness was the absence of Manasseh, from whom they were not likely to hear soon. And yet they gloried in knowing that Manasseh had chosen to meet tribulation for the sake of his faith, and that, wherever he was, he was helping others and fighting on the side of right.

"Father," said Mary, "how grand it is to be able to do something great and noble in the cause! Were I a man, I would go with Manasseh to fight for the Cross."

Nathan stroked her hair softly. "The life of everyone who is consecrated to God is directed by him," he said. "To Manasseh is given the privilege of defending the faith and helping the weak by his strong, young arm; to Mary is given the humble, loving life in which she may serve God just as truly and do just as great a work in faithfully performing her own little part. Think you not so, mother?"

"Ah, yes," returned the mother, with her gentle smile. "Life is like the cloth woven little by little, until the whole pattern shows in the finished work; and it matters not whether the pattern be large or small. So the little things of life, done well for Christ's sake, will at last make a noble whole of which none need be ashamed."

"But mother, watching the sheep, grinding the meal, washing the garments, seem such very little things."

"Yet all these are very necessary things," returned the mother quietly, "and if done cheerfully and willingly, call for an unselfish heart. A gentle, loving life lived amid little cares and trials is no small thing, my child."

Mary kissed her mother. "Mother, you always say what comforts one; you always make me wish to live more patiently and lovingly."

"And yet, Mary," said her father, "mother's life has been one round of small duties."

Mary sat thinking for a moment. "Yes, father," she answered slowly, "I see now that mother's life has been the very best sermon on duty. I shall try to be patient and happy in simply doing well whatever my hands find to do. But I wish Manasseh were home;" and she looked wistfully to the west, where bands of color were spreading up the sky, saffron at the horizon, blending into gold and tender green above, while all melted into a sapphire dome streaked and flecked with rosy pink rays and bars.

"How he would enjoy this glorious sunset! Oh, father, how dreadful if he were to be killed!—if he were nevermore to sit with us looking at the sunsets!" Her voice trembled a little as she spoke.

"We are committing him to the care of Almighty God," returned Nathan, solemnly. "God is love, and whatever he does will be best."

"You find great comfort, father, in believing that 'all things work together for good to them that love God,'" said Mary.

"For the children of God, everything that happens must be best."

"Even persecution and death?"

"Even persecution and death, if God so will."

Mary looked at his placid face for a long time, then she said: "How very peaceful you and mother are!"

"How could we be otherwise," the father replied, smiling, "with Jesus with us each hour, each moment? And we know that he 'will never leave nor forsake us.' I think, too, that he is very close to my daughter. Mary, is there anything in this world that could take the place of Jesus to you? Would wealth or honor or any earthly joy make you perfectly happy if you could never pray to Jesus more, never feel him near you as an ever-present Friend, nevermore have the hope of seeing his face?"

Mary clasped her hands, and her face glowed. "Never, oh, never!" she cried. "I would rather be like poor blind Bartimeus begging by the wayside, yet able to call, 'Jesus, Son of David, have mercy on me!'"

The sun had now set, and the sky had faded with that suddenness common in Eastern lands.

Nathan arose. "Let us now offer up prayer for the safety of Manasseh, and for the steadfastness of the brethren; for we know that where two or three are gathered together in Jesus' name, there is he in the midst of them. Let us pray!"

The three knelt in the dim chamber, with silence about and the evening stars above, and prayed for the lad who, amid very different scenes, was in the heart of the strange revolution. And then they sang the words of that sublime psalm, than which no grander poem was ever written:

> *I will lift up mine eyes unto the hills, from whence cometh my help.*
> *My help cometh from the Lord, which made heaven and earth.*
> *He will not suffer thy foot to be moved; he that keepeth thee will not slumber.*
> *Behold, he that keepeth Israel shall neither slumber nor sleep.*
> *The Lord is thy keeper; the Lord is thy shade upon thy right hand.*
> *The sun shall not smite thee by day, nor the moon by night.*
> *The Lord shall preserve thee from all evil; he shall preserve thy soul.*
> *The Lord shall preserve thy going out and thy coming in from this time forth, and even for evermore.*

CHAPTER XIX.

THE BATTLE OF OHOD.

"Dost thou not know the fate of soldiers?
They're but Ambition's tools, to cut a way
To her unlawful ends."
—Southern.

While these events had been taking place in the North, Henda had given Abu Sofian little peace, urging him every day to pay the dues of blood-revenge for her relatives, and taunting him with cowardice in his long delay.

At length, in the third year of the Hegira he gathered a considerable army, and with three thousand men of the Koreish tribe, among whom were two hundred horsemen, left Mecca, accompanied by Henda and fifteen of the matrons of Mecca bearing timbrels and singing warlike chants.

The whole army advanced with the intention of besieging Medina, but Mohammed's men entreated him to let them encounter Abu Sofian outside of the city, and he yielded to their entreaties. With only one thousand men,[10] fifty of whom were chosen archers, the prophet took up his stand on a declivity of Mount Ohod, about six miles north of the city. There, on its black and barren slope, he divided his army into four parts, three of which bore sacred banners, while the great standard was placed before Mohammed himself.

In order to imbue his men with courage, he came out in full view of the whole army, and, in a loud voice that penetrated even the farthest ranks, gave promise of victory. Then, for the sake of those who should be killed in battle, he expatiated upon the delights of that Paradise which surely awaited all who should be slain in the cause, representing it such a paradise as would be peculiarly adapted to the tastes and stimulating to the imagination of the Arabs—a race accustomed to arid wastes, burning sands, and glaring skies; a paradise of green fields and flowery gardens cooled by innumerable rivers and sparkling fountains, which glittered from between shaded bowers interwoven with perfumed

10   Burton gives seven hundred.

flowers. He gave them promise of streams literally flowing with milk and clearest honey; of trees bending with fruit which should be handed down by houris of wondrous beauty; he told them of treasures of gold, silver, and jewels. "They shall dwell in gardens of delight, reposing on couches adorned with gold and precious stones . . . . Upon them shall be garments of fine green silk and brocades, and they shall be adorned with bracelets of silver, and they shall drink of a most pure liquor—a cup of wine mixed with the water of Zenjebil, a fountain in Paradise named Salsabil."

Such was the sensual character of the paradise promised to his followers by Mohammed. The soldiers were listening eagerly to the words when the army of Abu Sofian was seen, advancing in the form of a crescent, with Abu Sofian and his idols in the center, and Henda and her women in the rear, sounding their timbrels, and singing loud war-chants.

The horsemen of the left wing of the Koreish now advanced to attack the Moslems in the flank, but the archers fired upon them from the top of some steep rocks, and they retired in confusion.

Hamza, a Moslem leader, then shouted the Moslem cry, "Death! Death!" and rushed down the hill upon the center. The crash and roar of battle began. High in air gleamed spear and lance; horses shrieked and reared, and tossed their long manes; dark, contorted visages and shining teeth shone out from clouds of dust; sashes floated on the air, and sabres flashed in the sunlight; all was mad confusion.

In the mêlée two young men met hand to hand. Both were tall and slight, and had dark, waving hair. So like were they that a warrior near them called out, "Behold, doth Manasseh fight with Manasseh!" But the youths heard not, recked not. Their blows fell thick and fast, until at last the Moslem gave way, and fell, wounded and bleeding, in the dust by the side of Hamza, who lay stiffening in death.

Then arose the shout, "The sword of God and his prophet!" and Abu Dudjana, armed with the prophet's own sword, waved it above his head and dashed into the thick of the battle.

Mosaab, the standard-bearer, followed close and planted the standard at the top of a knoll. An arrow struck him in the eye. He fell, and the cry arose that the prophet himself had fallen. Ali seized the standard and floated it aloft on the air; but the Moslems, seized with confusion, would not rally, and withdrew to the hilltop.

The Koreish, thinking Mohammed killed, forbore to follow

them, and began the revolting work of plundering the dead. Henda and her companions savagely assisted in the gruesome task; and, coming upon Hamza, the fierce woman mutilated his dead body.

By him she found the handsome youth, whom she believed to be Manasseh, so torn and covered with blood as to conceal his Moslem adornments. To Manasseh she had taken a strange fancy, and she now ordered the youth to be conveyed in safety to the camp, with the army which was forming in line of march.

The band of Jews who had come with the forces of Abu Sofian, mainly for the purpose of delivering those of their afflicted brethren who had refused to join Mohammed, and of whom many were imprisoned in Medina, now joined with a band of the Koreish, who desired the freedom of some of their tribe, and, while the excitement of battle was still fresh, the party entered the city by stealth, then, dashing furiously down the street to the guardhouse, overpowered the guards and battered open the doors, setting many of the prisoners free. Among these were Amzi, Asru, and Yusuf.

It was Manasseh himself who broke in the door of the apartment in which Yusuf was confined.

An exclamation of pleasure burst from him on recognizing the priest, and he threw his arms about his neck.

"Yusuf! My dear Yusuf!" he cried.

"My boy!" exclaimed the priest, in astonishment. "What means this?"

"It means that you are free," said the youth as he knocked off the chains. "Haste! We must on to the camp ere the Moslems return. Anything more than this I will tell you on the way."

Once again Yusuf stepped out into the pure air, along with many others who bore part of their chains in the broken links that still clanked upon their wrists and ankles.

In passing through the courtyard, the priest noticed some one crouched in a pitiable heap in a corner of the yard. Manasseh hauled him out. It was the peddler, with ashen face and eyes rolling with fear.

"Come along, my man!" laughed Manasseh. "Like the worm in a pomegranate, you are apt to do harm if left to yourself."

Abraham writhed and begged for mercy.

"Come along!" said Manasseh, impatiently. "I shall not hurt you; I shall merely look after you for awhile."

Thus consoled, the peddler hopped on with alacrity. A hasty mount was made and the party set out for the camp of Abu Sofian.

Yusuf then had a chance to ask the question burning at his heart. "How comes it, Manasseh, that you again fight against the prophet? When last I saw you, you wore the green of the Moslem."

"I!" said the youth in astonishment. "You jest, Yusuf!"

"It was surely you who met me on the field of Bedr."

"Yusuf, are you mad? It was never I."

"Then who can it have been? It was your very face."

"For once, Yusuf, your eyes have played you false. How could you have believed such a thing of Manasseh?"

"A strange resemblance!" mused Yusuf; then—"Whom see I before me yonder?"

"Manasseh's eyes do not play him false, and he declares it to be Amzi," said the youth.

They hastened up the narrow street, now crowded with soldiers, prisoners, camels, and horses; and, escaping the missiles thrown by infuriated Moslem women from the housetops, soon overtook Amzi and Asru. All proceeded at once to the camp of Abu Sofian.

Some large tents were set apart for the wounded Koreish, and here Yusuf and Amzi found speedy occupation in binding wounds, and giving drinks of water to the parched soldiers. Manasseh entered with them.

"What means this?" cried Henda. "Did I not have you conveyed, soaked with blood, among the wounded of the Koreish?"

"I have not been wounded today," returned Manasseh. "Read me this riddle, Henda. There must be a second self—"

"Here, Manasseh!" interrupted Yusuf from one side. "Had you a twin brother, this must be he."

Yusuf was bending over a youth whose dark eyes spoke of suffering, and who lay listlessly permitting the priest to bathe his blood-covered brow. His eyes were fixed on Manasseh, who was quickly coming forward, and those near wondered at the striking resemblance, more marked than is often found between brothers.

"Who are you, friend?" asked Manasseh, curiously.

"Kedar the Bedouin!" returned the youth, proudly. "Though how I came into a Koreish camp, is more than I can explain."

"For that you may thank your resemblance to me," laughed Manasseh. "You are weak, Kedar, my proud Bedouin, and we will ask you to talk but little; yet, I pray you, tell me, who was your father?"

"Musa, the Bedouin Sheikh,"—haughtily.

"And your mother was Lois, daughter of Eleazar?"

"Even so," returned the other, wonderingly.

"My cousin!" exclaimed Manasseh, delightedly seizing his hand.

"And son of my Bedouin friend, Musa!" exclaimed Yusuf.

So the Bedouin youth, the rash, hot-headed Moslem recruit, found himself among friends in a Koreish camp.

Night had now fallen, and under cover of darkness, Mohammed's army silently returned to Medina.

There were those who censured the prophet for his conduct at this battle; and some even dared to charge him with deception in promising them victory. But Mohammed told them that defeat was due to their sins: "Verily, they among you who turned their backs on the day whereon the two armies met at Ohod, Satan caused them to slip for some crime which they had committed."

To quiet those who lamented for their slain friends, he brought forth the doctrine that the time of every man's death is fixed by divine decree, and that he must meet it at that time, wherever he be.

In the morning the majority of Abu Sofian's forces set out for Mecca. Among them were Yusuf and Amzi, also Asru the captain; and it was with no small sense of comfort that the half starved prisoners sat again about Amzi's well-stocked board.

Manasseh was with them. Kedar, scorning to desert the Moslem army, had refused to leave Medina, and, by the earnest intercession of Yusuf and Amzi, whose word was of some import in Meccan ears, he had been given his freedom.

It was with deep relief that all felt the short respite from the blare of battle; and, though they looked forward to the future with anxious forebodings, and though their joy was clouded by the death of Dumah, they were thankful for present blessings. Not alone prayer, but praise, was an essential part of their religion, and their voices ascended in song,—

I will bless the Lord at all times; his praise shall continually be in thy mouth.

My soul shall make her boast in the Lord; the humble shall hear thereof, and be glad.

O magnify the Lord with me, and let us exalt his name together.

I sought the Lord, and he heard me, and delivered me from all my fears.

They looked unto him, and were lightened; and their faces were not ashamed.

This poor man cried, and the Lord heard him, and saved him out of all his troubles.

The angel of the Lord encampeth round about them that fear

him, and delivereth them.
*O taste and see that the Lord is good; blessed is the man that trust-
    eth in him.*
*O fear the Lord, ye his saints; for there is no want to them that
    fear him.*

CHAPTER XX.

THE BATTLE OF THE DITCH.

"Blood! blood! The leaves above me and around me
Are red with blood."

In the year which followed, Mohammed's forces were more than once directed against Syrian caravans, and the plunder divided among the Moslem troops after one-fifth had been appropriated by the prophet; but otherwise the truce was unbroken, until at the end of the year, the Koreish, uniting with neighboring tribes, many of whom were Jews, formed the plan of a grand attack which was to free El Hejaz forever from the power of the Islam despot.

From the Caaba the call was given to all who could be appealed to through religion, through the interests of commerce, or through desire for blood-revenge in consequence of the battles of Bedr and Ohod. To the more earnest Jews the undertaking took the form of a vast religious war, undertaken against the hosts of Satan for the deliverance of a land in bondage; to the Meccan merchants it assumed the guise of a commercial transaction which would again restore the trade so long ruined by Mohammed's hostile measures; to the Koreish and the desert tribes it seemed the grand opportunity of clearing the honor stained by the unrevenged death of their friends.

Accordingly a host of volunteers to the number of one hundred thousand offered themselves, and the vast array set out. Among the volunteers were Yusuf, Amzi, Asru, and the valiant Manasseh, all of whom deemed the necessity of the hour a sufficient reason for entering upon a course foreign to the laws of peace which they would fain have seen established.

A mighty host it seemed in a land whose battles had chiefly been confined to skirmishes between different tribes. As it wound its way down the narrow valley, the women of Mecca stood upon the housetops, listening to the trampling, and beseeching their household gods to bless the enterprise.

Long ere they reached Medina the prophet had received word of their advance, and had had a ditch or entrenchment dug about the city as a sort of fortification.

Abu Sofian ordered his tents to be pitched below on the plain, and, this done, he at once laid siege to the city.

But his bad generalship ruined the undertaking. For a month he kept his men wholly inactive, and during that time Mohammed busied himself in sending emissaries in the midst of Abu Sofian's men for the purpose of sowing disaffection among them; and so completely was this done that the besieging force became hollow and rotten to its core. Tribe after tribe left. The few faithful besought their leader to permit them to attack the city, and when at last the order was given, but a feeble remnant of the original host remained. Notwithstanding this, the command "Forward!" was hailed with tumultuous joy, and the besiegers pressed forward in irregular yet serried masses.

Scarcely had the attack begun when a terrific storm arose. It was in the winter season, and a sudden hurricane of cold winds came shrieking through the gaps of the mountains to the north.

Amzi, having, as an influential Meccan, been appointed to the command of a division, charged boldly forward in the teeth of the tempest, waving his sword above his head and cheering his men on with his hopeful voice. Yusuf, Asru and Manasseh pressed forward close behind him. A cloud of arrows met them, yet they poured impetuously on. And now the bank was climbed and the conflict became almost hand-to-hand. The priest's tall form rendered him conspicuous in the fray. Some one came hacking and hewing his way towards him. It was the agile Uzza. The priest was beset on all sides and was defending himself against fearful odds, when the face of Uzza, fiendlike in its hate, burst upon him as a new opponent. He raised his weapon for a blow, but the vision of a Guebre altar upon which a little, bleeding child lay, rose before him, and his arm fell.

Uzza perceived his advantage. With a howl of triumph he cried, "False priest, you shall not escape me this time!" and made a fierce stroke with his scimitar. But the blow was parried.

"Simpleton! Would you let him kill you?" cried a harsh voice close by the priest. And the next moment Uzza fell with a death-groan at the feet of Asru.

And now the storm struck with full fury, howling among the houses of Medina, whistling shrilly on the upper air, and bending the palm trees low along its furious path. Thatches were torn from the roofs and carried whirling through the air; clouds of dust were blown high along the streets, and black, ragged clouds scurried across the sky as if urged on by demon-force. Horses neighed loudly. Many of them became unmanageable, and dashed, with terrified eyes and distended nostrils, through the midst of the flying soldiery. The tents of Abu Sofian were torn from their pegs and hurled away. Then the rain descended in sheets, or, whirled round by the wind, swirled along in columns with almost the force of a waterspout.

Suddenly a cry was raised: "It is Mohammed! The prophet has raised the storm by enchantment!"

The cry echoed from mouth to mouth above the roar of the tempest. The superstitious Arabs were seized with terror and fled precipitately, believing themselves surrounded by legions of invisible spirits. Amzi and his little band stayed until the last; then, deserted by all and blinded by the descending torrents, they, too, were obliged to withdraw, and another victory, that of the Battle of the Ditch, had fallen to the prophet.

This was the last expedition undertaken by the Koreish against their victorious enemy. Mohammed, of course, attributed his great conquest to divine agency. In a passage from the Koran he declared:

"O true believers, remember the favor of God toward you, when armies of infidels came against you, and we sent against them a wind and hosts of angels which ye saw not."

The heart sickens in following further Mohammed's willful career of blood. During the following five years he is said to have commanded twenty-seven expeditions and fought nine pitched battles. Against the Christian Jews in particular the bitterest expressions of his hate were directed; and to his dying day this incomprehensible man, from whose lips proceeded words of mercy and of deadliest rancor, words of love and of hate, words of purity and of gross sensuality—this strange man persecuted them to the last, nor ever ceased to direct his arms against all who followed that gentle Jesus of Nazareth of whose power this blood-marked, self proclaimed prophet of Allah was envious.

His followers, dazzled by the glare of his brilliant victories or solicitous for self preservation, constantly swelled in numbers, but there were a few who, like Kedar, had heard of the peaceableness of the religion of Jesus Christ, and who began to sicken of the flow of blood which deluged the sands of El Hejaz, and ran even into the Nejd, the borders of Syria, and of Arabia-Felix.

Kedar often longed for the friendly touch, the hearty, kindly words, of the friends whom he had met and parted from as in a dream. He had soon refused to believe in Mohammed's divine appointment. Even this Bedouin youth had enough penetration to see that religion must stand upon its results, and that the private life of Mohammed would not stand the test of inspection. Fain would he have left his ranks many and many a time. The brand of coward he knew could not be attached to him for leaving victorious ranks to ally himself with the few and feeble Jews, yet there was something in the idea of "turning his coat" which he did not like. He imagined in a vague way that such a proceeding would compromise his principles of honor, and he had not reached the wisdom of that great educator, Comenius, who, not long ere his death, wrote a treatise upon "the art of wisely withdrawing one's own assertions." So he fought doggedly on, until circumstances again threw him into the bosom of his friends.

CHAPTER XXI.

THE FAMILY OF ASRU.

"God's in his heaven, all's right with the world."

On the evening upon which the Battle of the Ditch was fought, the wife of Asru, and his daughter, Sherah, now almost grown to womanhood, were returning from performing Tawaf at the temple. They had prayed for the success of the Koreish expedition; they had drank of the well of Ismael, Zem-Zem, and had poured its water on their heads. Now they were hastening home to offer prayers to their household gods in the same cause, for, during Asru's apostasy to the Moslem ranks, his wife, a woman of the Koreish, and her family had never swerved from their hostility to Mohammed and all connected with him. For their obstinacy in this, they had been cruelly abused by Asru, who, with the superiority which most men in the East assume over women, ruled as a tyrant in his house.

It was with unspeakable satisfaction that Sherah and her mother found that Asru had at last broken all connection with the prophet, but a change had come into his manner which was to them most unaccountable. Instead of cruelty now was kindness; instead of stormy petulance, now was patience; and yet, Asru had not mentioned the cause of his new life. A sort of backwardness on the subject, a desire to know more of it before communicating with others, strove with him against the dictates of his conscience, and he had as yet been dumb. He had not concealed his connection with the little band of Jewish Christians. In spite of the jeers of his friends among the Koreish, he had attended their meetings regularly. That had been the extent of his active Christian work; yet his life had been preaching while his lips were still.

Sherah and her mother talked of him as they walked.

"Mother, however it be, father was never kind until he went to the Jewish meetings."

"True. Yet many of these same Jews are wicked, thieves, low robbers, not fit for such as Asru to mingle with," said the mother haughtily.

"Yet not the Jews who attend the church," returned the girl, quickly. "I know them. Most of them are poor, but not thieves; they seem quiet, industrious people. Then, Amzi attends there now, you know, and Yusuf, who, when the plague was raging, spent weeks in attending the sick. Did he not come to father and sit with him night after night, when, mother—I shame to say it—both you and I fled!"

The mother walked in silence for a moment.

"There must be some strange power that urges a man to do such acts," she said, musingly. "It would be easier far to go out to battle, urged on by the enthusiasm of conquest, and cheered by the music and clash of timbrels to deeds of bravery. It takes a different spirit to enter the houses of filthy disease, to court death in reeking lazar-houses, to sit for weeks watching hideous faces and listening to the ravings of madmen through the long, hot nights of the plague-season."

"Mother, I am convinced that their religion prompts them to do it. What else can it be?"

"What is their religion?"

"I know not; yet we may know for the going, perhaps. See, the lights gleam in their little hall. They hold meeting tonight. Let us go."

"What! And let the proud tribe of the Koreish, the guardians of the Caaba, see a woman of the Koreish enter there?"

"We can go in long cloaks, mother, and it is well-nigh dark. Come, will you not?"

The pleading voice was so earnest that the mother consented. Yet, that the influence of the gods in the result of the battle might not be lost, they first entered their own house, prostrated themselves before the gods, and besought their aid in the Koreish cause. Then, donning long outer cloaks, and veiling their faces closely, the two slipped out of a back way and stealthily hastened towards the Jewish church.

It was late when they arrived. Neither Yusuf nor Amzi was present to raise the hearts of their hearers with words of simple and earnest piety, no voice of Manasseh was there to lead in the songs of praise, but an old man with snowy hair and a saintlike face was standing behind a table, a volume of the Scriptures before him, and the voices of the congregation, some twenty in number, arose in the old, yet ever new words:

"The Lord is my shepherd, I shall not want. He maketh me to lie down in green pastures; he leadeth me beside the still waters. He restoreth my soul: he leadeth me in the paths of righteousness for his name's sake. Yea, though I walk through the valley of the shadow of death, I will fear no evil, for thou art with me; thy rod and thy staff they comfort me."

The Koreish woman listened. She could not understand all

this. Yet it was beautiful,—"green pastures," "still waters." Could it be that these people knew of an Elysian spot, unknown to Meccans—that their God led them to such favored retreats? She could restrain her impatience no longer.

"Where are the green pastures and still waters?" she cried, impetuously, "that I too may go to them!"

The old man smiled with serene kindness. "Daughter," he said, "the green pastures and still waters are the pleasant places of the soul. Hast thou never known what it was to have doubts and fears, restlessness and dissatisfaction in the present, uncertainty for the future, a feeling that there is little in life, and a great gulf in death?"

"I have felt so almost every day," she replied, passionately.

"Hast thou not found comfort in thy gods?" he asked, gently.

"Alas, I fear to say that I have not!" she exclaimed.

"And why fearest thou thus?" he said.

"Ah, knowest thou not that the gods are gods of vengeance?" she replied in an awed whisper.

"I know naught of your gods," he returned. "Our God is a God of love. He gives us the certainty of his presence ever with us in this life, his companionship in death, and the privilege of looking upon his face and being 'forever with the Lord' in the world to come."

"And are you not afraid of death?" she asked. "To me it seems a dreadful thing. It makes me shudder to think that I too must one day suffer the struggle for breath, and then lie still and cold."

"To those who love the Lord 'to die is gain,'" he said. "Have we not sung 'Yea, though I walk through the valley of the shadow of death, I will fear no evil, for Thou art with me'? Surely one who believes that, and knows that he is going to be always with the Lord, always able to look on his face, need not fear death."

"It is a beautiful thought," the woman said, bowing her head on her hands.

"Yet not more beautiful than the thought that the Holy Spirit is ever with us; that Jesus himself is our brother, and understands all our little troubles; that he has promised to help us in overcoming all evil. 'For every one that asketh receiveth, and he that seeketh findeth, and to him that knocketh it shall be opened.' 'If a son shall ask bread of any of you that is a father, will he give him a stone? If he ask a fish, will he for a fish give him a serpent? Or if he shall ask an egg, will he offer him a scorpion? If ye, then, being evil, know how to give good gifts to your children, how much more shall your heavenly Father give the Holy Spirit to them that ask him.' Daughter, these are the very words of Jesus. Do they not show you the way to the still waters and green pastures? Do you not see that the love of our God acts upon the heart as gentle showers upon the barren land, causing it to rejoice and bring forth fruit worthy of being presented to our Lord and Master? 'He hath loved us with an everlasting love.' He loves us ever, therefore in our returning this love to him doth the 'peace of God that passeth all understanding' lay hold upon our hearts."

"But ye are Jews!" she said. "Such promises are not for the Koreish."

"Such promises are for all," was the confident reply. "Jesus said whosoever believeth in him should not perish, but have everlasting life. None so sinful that Jesus cannot wash out the stain; none are excluded from his mercy. Daughter, believe, receive. Let the love of God enter thine heart, and repent best by doing thine evil deeds no more. Only come to Jesus himself. Only have faith in him."

The Koreish woman hid her face in her hands again, and answered nothing. The old man turned to the Scriptures and read the story of Jesus and the woman of Samaria, raising his voice in triumphant fervor as he reached the words: "Whosoever drinketh of the water that I shall give him shall never thirst; but the water that I shall give him shall be in him a well of water springing up into everlasting life."

Then he turned to the words spoken by Jesus to his disciples just before his betrayal, and read: "Peace I leave with you; my peace I give unto you. Let not your heart be troubled," and, "Abide in me, and I in you. As the branch cannot bear fruit of itself except it abide in the vine, no more can ye except ye abide in me. I am the vine, ye are the branches; he that abideth in me, and I in him, the same bringeth forth much fruit; for without me ye can do nothing."

The woman listened. With the quick appreciation of the Arab for metaphor and simile, she grasped the meaning of the words, and a new, wonderful train of thought came into her mind as she sat with bowed head while simple, pleading, heart-offered prayer was sent up to the Throne of Grace, and the parting hymn was sung.

Then the little band gathered around her, speaking words of cheer, and the aged leader dismissed her with a gentle, "Come again, daughter."

As Sherah and her mother walked home, the last remnant of the fearful storm that had visited Medina passed over Mecca.

They saw the ragged clouds borne wildly over the northern hills; they saw the stunted aloes bending low beneath the sweep of the wind. Yet to them there was a grandeur in it, for there was still upon them the influence of the Divine presence, and they thought of Him who "walketh upon the wings of the wind."

And as they went on, bowing their heads before its spent fury, Asru, Amzi, and Yusuf, far to the northward, struggled on with the fugitive army, wondering at the continued triumph of the false prophet, yet serene in the confidence that in the Divine Hands all was well, and that in the far-distant end, however blurred to human vision, all must work for good to those who love God, even though the reason of his working, the seeming mystery of the fortunes of the great conflict, might not be unravelled until in the bright hereafter, when all things will at last be made plain.

CHAPTER XXII.

MANASSEH AND ASRU AT KHAIBAR.

"Spirit of purity and grace,
Our weakness, pitying, see!
O make our hearts thy dwelling-place,
And worthier Thee."

The Koreish, after their disastrous defeat at the Battle of the Ditch, returned in bitter disappointment to Mecca. Many even of the bravest of the tribe felt that it was hopeless to strive against the prophet, whose phenomenal success seemed to render his troops invincible. Many, too, with the superstition at all times common to the Arabs, were in deadly dread of his "enchantments," and were only too ready to listen to his bold assertions that the momentous storm at the siege of Medina had been caused in his favor by heavenly agency; that a great host of angels had been in invisible cooperation with the Moslems and had drawn their legions about the ill-fated company, crying, "God is great!" and striking panic to the hearts of the besiegers.

Because of these superstitions the hearts of the Arabs failed them, and they day after day lessened in their hostility, and increased in their spirit of submission to the now famous prophet of El Islam.

The Jews, however, held out to the last, and against them the reeking blades of Mohammed's army were turned. The Jewish tribes of the Koraidha, Kainoka, and the Nadhirites, in the vicinity of Medina, were speedily overthrown, and their goods taken possession of by the Moslems. Then, before the blood cooled on the scimitars, these conquests were followed by the dastardly assassination of the few Jews who were still in Medina, and, being possessed of considerable property, were a tempting bait to the avaricious prophet, who now, making religion a cloak to cover his greed and ambition, went to the wildest excesses in attaining his objects.

Many of the Jews, escaping dearly with their lives, fled to the city of Khaïbar, five days' journey to the northeast of Medina, a city inhabited by Jews, who, living in the midst of a luxuriant farming district, had grown rich in the peaceful arts of agriculture and commerce. Others hastened thither in the hope that Khaïbar might become the nucleus of a successful resistance of Mohammed's power in the near future; and among the latter class was Manasseh.

Late one afternoon he arrived in the rich pasturelands surrounding the city. The air of peace and prosperity, the lowing of herds and bleating of sheep, delighted him; and, though weary from his journey, it was with a light heart that he urged his flagging horse between the long groves of palm trees until the city came in sight.

His martial spirit glowed as he noted the heavy outworks, and the strength of the citadel Al Kamus, which, built on a high rock, and towering ragged and black against the orange sky of the setting sun, seemed to the young soldier almost impregnable.

He was welcomed at the gates as another recruit to the gathering forces, and, on his request, was at once directed to the house of the chief, Kenana Ibn al Rabi, a man reputed to be exceedingly wealthy. Here he was courteously received by Kenana and his wife Safiya; and, in a long conference, he informed the chief of the numbers and zeal of Mohammed's army, urging upon him the immediate strengthening of the city, as it was highly probable that the prophet would not long desist from making an attempt upon a tidbit so tempting as that which Khaïbar presented.

That evening an informal council of war was held in the courtyard of the chief's house. Al Hareth, a brother of Asru, a man who, although an Arab, had been appointed to high office, and had proved himself one of the most distinguished commanders of the Jewish colony, was present; and, among others, Asru himself entered.

"Asru!" exclaimed Manasseh, delightedly, hurrying him aside to an arbor, "you here! I thought I had become separated from you all in that ill-fated storm. Where are Amzi and Yusuf, know you?"

"Gone to Mecca with Abu Sofian's remnant of an army—as miserable and hang-head lot of fugitives as ever disgraced field!" said Asru contemptuously. "By my faith, it shamed me to see our brave friends in their company, even for the journey!"

"Why did they go to Mecca?"

"Because they were firmly convinced that Mecca will be the next point of attack," said Asru, "but methinks they shall find themselves mistaken. Mohammed will keep Mecca as a sort of sacred spot, dedicated to his worship—and the worship of Allah!" with infinite scorn. "But Khaïbar is a pomegranate of the highest branches, too mellow, too luscious, too tempting, to elude his grasp. Yes, Manasseh, Khaïbar will be his next point of attack.

However, I am truly glad that Yusuf and Amzi have gone home. The Jews and Christians in Mecca will be safe enough for some time to come, and our friends are getting too old to endure much fatigue of battle."

"Aye, Asru, you and I are better fitted to face the brunt of the charge and the weariness of the march. The work of Yusuf and Amzi should be milder, though not less glorious, than ours."

"You say well," returned the other, with kindling eye. "Asru, for one, can never forget what they have done for him."

"Asru, are all the stories of the wickedness of your past life—your cruelty, your treachery, your blasphemy—true?"

"Manasseh, let my past life go into the tomb of oblivion if you will. 'Tis a sorry page for Asru to look upon. The cruelty, the blasphemy,—aye, boy, I was full of it; but treacherous, never! Whatever Asru was, and no devil was blacker than he in many ways, he was never guilty of perfidy, except you call the trying to free Amzi and poor Dumah perfidy."

"I am glad," returned Manasseh, quietly; "yet it would not matter now, since our Asru is a changed man."

Asru looked at the youth earnestly. "Manasseh," he said, "does the old nature never come back upon you? Or have you never known what it was to feel wrong impulses?"

"Wrong impulses!" exclaimed the other. "Yes, Asru, many and many a time. Yet, when one does not even look at the evil, but keeps his face turned steadfastly towards the right, the old self seems to lose its hold. In drawing near to God we draw away from evil."

"Your words, I know, are true," returned the other; "yet the keeping from doing wrong seems to me the hardest thing in living a Christian life."

"But, Asru," said Manasseh, "perhaps you are not loving enough. The more you love Jesus, and the more you feel him in your life, the easier it will be to turn from temptation—to hate the thing that inspires it. If you really love him you simply cannot do what will pain him."

"But the temptation to act hastily, to speak unkindly, comes upon me so often, Manasseh, that I grow discouraged."

"The only safety is in always looking Above for help. Believe me, Asru, I speak from experience. Temptation in itself is not sin; the yielding to it is. Little by little the temptations bother us less, and we grow in grace. You know this is expected of us. Paul speaks of 'perfecting holiness in the fear of the Lord.' He says, too, 'The weapons of our warfare are not carnal, but mighty through God to the pulling down of strongholds.' He said, also, to the Philippians, 'It is God that worketh in you, both to will and to do of his good pleasure,' and the Lord himself has said, 'My grace is sufficient for you, for my strength is made perfect in weakness.' So, Asru, my friend, the whole secret is in accepting that gift, in knowing him, and in keeping the soul in a constant state of openness for the working of the Holy Spirit—a 'pray-without-ceasing' attitude in which one's whole life is resolved into the prayer: 'Thy will, not mine, be done.'"

Asru regarded Manasseh curiously.

"How is it, young as you are," he said, "that these things are so plain to you?"

"Ah, you forget," said Manasseh, "what a blessed home training I have had, and that from my childhood I have had Yusuf for my counsellor. For these Christian friends of my childhood, I never cease to be thankful."

Asru turned his face away. "And I, too, have children, Manasseh," he said in a low voice, "children who, with their mother, are little better than idolaters, and I have never told them differently."

"But you will teach them?" returned Manasseh.

"Ah, yes, if God spares me through this perilous time I shall teach them."

"Have you heard or seen aught of Kedar, lately?" asked Manasseh, abruptly.

"In the Battle of the Ditch I saw him for a moment, charging furiously against one of Abu Sofian's divisions. He was in advance of the rest, riding with his head bent in the teeth of the tempest. On a knoll above me, I saw him for a moment, between me and the sky, his hair and long sash streaming in the wind; then the rain came, and I saw him no more. Aye, but he is a brave lad!"

"Poor cousin!" said Manasseh. "It is misplaced bravery. Would he were one of us!"

"He is not a Christian; and, unless he were so, a spirit like his would scorn to be one of such a craven, contention-torn mob as that which Abu Sofian brought to the field. Strange, is it not, that the little band of Christians find themselves allied to a set of idolaters, against one who would cast idols down?"

"Aye, but Mohammed would trample Christians and idolaters alike. Think you that defeat was owing wholly to cowardice of the soldiers?"

"Not so much, perhaps, as to bad generalship of the leader," returned Asru. "Nevertheless the superstition of the heathen

Arabs, and their fear when the cry of Mohammed's enchantment was raised, made a craven of every one of them. Manasseh, had we had ten thousand Christian Jews, there might have been a different story."

"We are nearly all Jews, here," said Manasseh, proudly. "Have you happy forebodings for the issue of the next combat?"

Asru shook his head, gloomily. "There will be a brave resistance on the part of our garrisons," he said, "although many of the men are well-nigh as ignorant and superstitious as the heathen Arabs; but Mohammed's forces have swelled wondrously since the 'enchanted' storm. Well, we can but do our best. Now, I see that the council has assembled. They call us. Come."

The two left the arbor and joined the others in the middle of the garden. And there, while the stars shone peacefully above in the evening sky, and the palm trees waved, and a little bird twittered contentedly over its nest in an olive bush, these men talked of measures of fortification, of tactics of war, and schemes of bloodshed; a conversation forced upon them, not as a matter of choice but of necessity—the necessity of a desperate few, earthed by a relentless conqueror and a ruthless despot, whose intolerance to all who denied his claims has never been surpassed in earth's history.

CHAPTER XXIII.

MOHAMMED'S PILGRIMAGE.

"Five great enemies to peace inhabit with us, viz.: Avarice, Ambition, Envy, Anger, and Pride."
—Petrarch.

In the meantime Yusuf and Amzi had taken up the old routine of life in Mecca—the faithful doing of the daily round, the little deeds of charity, the duties of business, the attendance at meetings in the little church. Everything seemed to sink back into the old way, yet there was not a man in the city but held himself in readiness to take up arms were an attack made upon them to wrest from them their freedom.

And word came that Mohammed was coming,—coming, not in war, but in peace, on his first pilgrimage to the Caaba. Mecca was instantly thrown into the wildest confusion. Some deemed the prophet's message honorable, but the majority were dubious, and thought that if Mohammed once gained an entrance, notwithstanding the fact that it was the sacred month Doul Kaada, his coming would be but to deluge the streets with blood.

A hasty consultation was held, and a troop of horse under one Khaled Ibn Waled, was sent out to check the prophet's advance. Mohammed, however, by means of his spies, early got word of this sally, and, turning aside from the way, he proceeded by ravines and bypaths through the mountains; and, ere the Meccans were aware of his proximity, his whole force was encamped near the city.

A deputation came from his army to the dignitaries of Mecca bearing messages of peace; but their reception was haughty.

"Go to him who sent you," was the reply to their overtures, "and say that Meccan doors are shut to one against whom every family in Mecca owes the revenge of blood."

For days the deputation was sent, with the same result, until at last ambassadors of the prophet entered with the offer of a truce for ten years.

The promise of a long respite from blood, and the hope of securing time to recuperate their forces, caught the ear of the Meccans. A deputation was appointed to treat with the prophet, and Amzi, though a Christian, by reason of his wisdom and learning was chosen as one of the representatives.

Yusuf accompanied him to an eminence above the defile in which the Moslem tents were pitched. A strange sight it was. Far as eye could reach, tents, white and black, dotted the narrow valley; horses were picketed, and camels browsed; and in the foreground one thousand four hundred men were grouped, waiting to hear the issue of the conference,—one thousand four hundred men, barefooted, and with shaven heads, and each wearing the white skirt and white scarf over the shoulder, assumed by pilgrims. Strangely different were they from the ordinary troops of the prophet, strangely unrecognizable in their garb of humility and peace; yet a second glance revealed the fact that each carried a sheathed sword.

Yusuf remained above, but Amzi descended with the embassy sent with the message that the treaty, if suitable, would be at once ratified. Mohammed, who, in place of his green garb, now with obsequious humility wore the pilgrims' costume, expressed his pleasure at the amicable attitude of the Meccans. He was seated upon a white camel named El Kaswa in honor of the faithful beast which had borne him in the earlier vicissitudes of his fortunes. Beside him, at a table placed on the sand, sat his vizier and son-in-law, Ali, to whom was given the task of writing the treaty as dictated by Mohammed.

"Begin, O Ali," said the prophet, "'In the name of the most merciful God'—"

Sohail, the spokesman of the Meccan deputation, immediately objected, "It is the custom of the Meccans to begin, 'In Thy name, O God.'"

"So be it," assented the prophet; then, continuing, he dictated the opening of the body of the treaty—"'These are the conditions on which Mohammed, the apostle of God, has made peace with those of Mecca.'"

A deep murmur of disapproval arose throughout the Meccan embassy.

"Not so, O Mohammed!" cried Sohail again. "Had we indeed acknowledged you as the prophet of God, think you we would have sent Khaled Ibn Waled with armed men against you? Think you we would have closed the streets of Mecca against one whom we recognized as an ambassador of the Most High? No, Mohammed, son of Abdallah, it must not be 'apostle of God.'"

Mohammed again bowed in token of submission. "Write thus, then, O Ali," he said. "'These are the conditions on which Mohammed, son of Abdallah, has made peace with those of Mecca.'"

He then proceeded to the terms of the treaty, stipulating that the prophet and his followers should have access to the city at any season during the period of truce, provided they came unarmed, habited as pilgrims, and did not remain over three days at a time.

This business concluded, the embassy from Mecca retraced its way; and Mohammed, changing his mind about entering the city at that time, ordered that prayers should be offered up on the spot, that seventy camels should there be sacrificed, and that the pilgrims should then return home.

This was accordingly done, and the people went back in some disappointment to Medina, where the prophet announced the success of his mission in a new passage from the Koran:

"Now hath God verified unto his apostle the vision wherein he said, Ye shall surely enter the holy temple of Mecca, if God please, in full security."

CHAPTER XXIV.

THE SIEGE OF KHAIBAR.—KEDAR.

"The drying up a single tear has more of honest fame than shedding seas of gore."

In the same year, the seventh year of the Hejira, Mohammed made the expected attack on Khaïbar. The chief, Kenana, got word of his approach, and ordered that the country for miles around the capital should be laid waste. For days the long roads leading into the city from every direction, swarmed with a moving line of anxious faced people, driving their camels and sheep ahead of them, and leading mules laden with household property. Low wagons creaked beneath the weight of fodder for the animals, and corn and dates for the people; and the loud "Yákh! Yákh!" of the camel-drivers mingled with the thud of the camel-sticks falling upon the thick hides of the lazy animals.

Asru was given charge of the expedition for laying waste the country; and never was a more considerate destroyer.

"Here, here!" he would cry to an aged man, "let me load that animal for you!" and he would lift the heavy burden to the back of the packmule, while the old man would say, "You are surely a kind soldier after all."

"I will carry this sick girl," he would say, to another, and would lift her as gently as a mother and place her in the shugduf in which she was to be conveyed to the city.

His spirit of gentleness spread among his men.

"Let us be kind to our friends, men," he would urge upon them. "The day is fast coming when we can scarcely be kind to our enemies, be we never so willing."

So the people, though sad as they looked back upon their smouldering homes and blazing palm trees, were filled with love for the gentle soldiers, and went up with a new motive in striking for their liberty, for there is naught that will bring forth the strongest powers of action like the impulse of love.

Ah, the blight and misery of war! Manasseh looked out from the citadel upon the scene which he had deemed so fair—the waving cornfields, the groves of palms and olives and aloes, the nestling houses, the pastures covered with flocks—now but a blackened and smoking waste, with here and there the skeleton of a palm tree pointing upward like a bony finger; and here and there a reeking column of black smoke, or the dull glare of a burning homestead.

The people murmured not. "Better let it lie in ashes than permit it to fall into the hands of the impostor!" they cried, and they muttered curses upon the head of the destroyer of their happiness and prosperity.

All were at last in and the anxious waiting began. Keen eyes peered from the citadel night and day. Watchmen were posted at every point of the outworks and spies were sent broadcast through the country.

Then the fateful word came. Breathless scouts told of an army fast approaching, twelve hundred men and two hundred horse, commanded by the prophet himself, his vizier Ali, and his friend Abu Beker.

Al Kamus, the citadel, was immediately crowded with men, and soldiers were posted along the walls, neither strong in numbers nor in arms, for many were armed but with staves and stones. Desperation was in their hearts, and calm, resolute faces looked forth for the advancing host.

Just as the morning sun flashed defiantly from the towers of Al Kamus, the Moslem army came in sight. At first it seemed like a moving, shapeless mass over the blackened fields,—and as the rising sun fell upon it, the moving mass became dotted with glints and lines of silver, like the ripple of waves on a sunlit sea; but the watchers recognized the deadly import of those bright gleams, and by the flash of scimitars and lances were able to compute in a vague way the strength of their opponents.

On they came until the stony place called Mansela was reached, and there, beneath a great rock, the host halted. The anxious watchers from the city could not discern the exact meaning of this, but more than one guessed that the halt was made for the offering of ostentatious prayer by the prophet.

This indeed was the case. As Mohammed came in full view of the citadel he cried out: "There, O believers, is the eyrie to which ye must climb. But victory has been promised us. Angels shall again lend us their invisible aid. Therefore have courage, O believers! Remember that for each of those vile infidels slain, a double joy awaits you in paradise. Know ye that every drop of an unbelieving Jew shed is as the crystal drops of nectar of paradise to the happy follower of Mohammed, the prophet of God. And fear not that ye be slain in this combat, O faithful! Ye will not be slain except your appointed time has come, when ye must in any case die. Remember that to be slain in battle for the cause of Islam is to reap a glorious reward!"

Then, mounting the great rock, he called with a loud voice: "La illaha il Allah! Mohammed Resoul Allah!" (There is no God but God! Mohammed is the prophet of God!)

And while the fanatics below prostrated themselves he prayed long and loudly.

Then the tents were pitched and the siege began. For many days it lasted. So abundant had been the supplies of food, and so numerous the droves of animals brought into the city, that those within the walls had no fear of famine. But so complete was the devastation of the country that the prophet's troops began to suffer for want of food. Yet they waited, as a suitable time of attack had not arrived. In the meantime they were engaged in digging trenches as a protection to the troops.

Manasseh and Asru were much together. They had become like brothers, and night after night they met on the citadel and looked out over the strange scene that was presented to the inhabitants of Khaïbar every evening during the siege. For, daily, just as the sun was setting, the whole Moslem army, with the prophet praying loudly at its head, set out in solemn procession, then proceeded round and round the city until seven circuits were completed, as in Tawaf at the Caaba.

Many among the more superstitious Jews of Khaïbar and their few Koreish adherents felt a thrill of awe as they looked upon this ceremony, fearing that the prophet was again practicing his arts of enchantment upon them; but the performance never failed to bring the smile of scorn to Asru's lips.

"Blind fanatics!" he exclaimed one evening. "A precious set of idiots!"

But Manasseh looked serious. "Asru," he said, "of course, I do not believe in all this; yet there is a something solemn in it to me. It makes me think of the seven circuits made about Jericho, when the priests blew upon the trumpets and the walls fell."

"Ah, but the voice of Jehovah gave the order then; now,"—and he smiled contemptuously—"the commanding voice is that of Mohammed, the peaceful Meccan trader, anon the gentle prophet of Allah, anon the bloodthirsty vulture and cutthroat robber, destroyer of life and liberty."

"Verily, Asru the Moslem soldier has completely changed," returned Manasseh, smiling.

"Aye, Manasseh, thanks to the peaceful Gospel of Jesus, Asru the Moslem, the lover of war, would now fain see this fair land smiling with happy homes and peaceful tillers of the soil. What is that about the child and the cockatrice?"

"'And the sucking child shall play on the hole of the asp, and the weaned child shall lay its hand on the cockatrice' den. They shall not hurt nor destroy in all my holy mountain; for the earth shall be full of the knowledge of the Lord, as the waters cover the sea,'" quoted Manasseh solemnly.

Asru looked thoughtfully out towards the distant hills, but he did not see them. He saw a quiet home in Mecca, where a pale-faced wife, a beautiful daughter, and two bright-eyed boys, sat.

"Manasseh," he said at length, "it may be that I shall be killed in this battle. If I am and you are spared, go to my wife and children. Tell them the Gospel for me. My great regret is that I myself put it off until too late. Will you, Manasseh?"

Manasseh pressed his friend's hand warmly. "You may trust me, if I live," he said simply. And the soldier was satisfied.

"Manasseh, I am rich," he continued. "See that my wealth is used for the best."

Manasseh pressed his hand again, and the tall soldier left him, feeling that, whatever happened, this young man's fidelity and integrity could be depended upon.

And now the Moslem army began to weary of inaction. Several desultory attacks were made by them, and batteringrams were set in play against the walls, but with no effect, until a grand attempt was decided upon. Night had scarcely faded into morning, and the rock of Mansela still stood black and shapeless against a gray sky, when a commotion was seen in the Moslem camp. Mohammed's troops no longer made the wild onslaught of untrained Bedouin hordes. The experience of scores of engagements had taught their leader the necessity of system; and now the host began to move in regular order in three main divisions. Above the center one floated the sacred flag of the prophet; to the right waved Ali's standard, a design of the sun; and to the left fluttered the Black Eagle of Abu Beker's division.

The battle began by an assault led by Abu Beker. Scaling-ladders were placed, and the Moslems swarmed up the walls, but a desperate band led by Al Hareth met them, and the besieging party, after a sharp fight, was compelled to withdraw. Shouts of triumph and jeers of derision arose from the city walls. The Moslems were frantic. Cries of vengeance were heard from their ranks.

Then Ali, shouting, "For God and the prophet!" dashed forward. He was dressed in scarlet, and wore a cuirass of steel. Over his head he waved the prophet's sword, and at the head of his division floated a sacred banner. Straight on he dashed towards a breach in the wall, and there, on a pile of loose stones, he fixed the standard.

Al Hareth rushed to the fore, and a desperate, singlehanded combat ensued. The Moslem army and the garrison of the city alike held their breath. The contest was unequal. In a moment Al Hareth had fallen, and a mighty cheer burst from the prophet's men.

Manasseh was stationed at the head of a band of horsemen, whom he was now with difficulty keeping in check. Yet for a moment he forgot all in watching a figure that was ascending the breach.

Whose but Asru's that gigantic form? Whose but Asru's that floating turban of white—that helmet in which flashed a diamond placed there by Kenana's own hand? Whose but Asru's that clanking sword and that three-pronged spear which none but he could wield?

"Surely now the Moslem will waver!" thought the youth; and with bated breath he watched this second combat, waged beside the bleeding form of Asru's dead brother.

With dauntless air the Moslem awaited the coming of Asru. They closed upon each other. The armies looked on, motionless, breathless, the combatants struggled, a writhing mass, broken only by the flash of the spear and glitter of the lance, as deadly blows were dealt or parried—and the sunshine rained from above. The very air seemed to stand still in watching, and the clash of every stroke was borne, with painful distinctness, to the ears of Asru's friend.

The combat was an equal one, Ali's agility matching well the superior strength of his antagonist, and it was not soon over. At last the Moslem seemed to stagger.

There, there, Asru, strike! He falls, he falls! There is your advantage! Strike! Joy, joy! victory is ours!

But no! Ye gods, what is wrong! Why stands Asru there, helpless? Why does he not act? By Allah, he loses time! Ha! his turban end has become twisted over his eyes beneath his helmet! Help! Help! Ye gods! Ha! Ali rises with a sharp recoil! He strikes! Woe! Woe! Asru is down!

A shout breaks afresh from the Moslem army as the brave Asru's body is dragged to one side of the breach. And now the Moslems dash forward like an avalanche. The breach widens; the green and yellow turbans swarm within the walls. Manasseh's horse dash forward. Over the open square a detachment of Moslem horse is spurring, the horsemen bending low as they ride, their maddened animals, gorgeous in trappings of scarlet, yellow and blue, with tails knotted at the ends, "like unto the heads of serpents." With regular sway the long spears swing with the motion of the horses.

Clash! The opposing forces meet. Men fall. Horses roll over in the dust. Back! Back! The Moslems are in headlong flight! Yet one youth fights on. Straight for the young Jewish leader he dashes. Blows rain on each side. Some of the Jewish horse close round.

"Keep off, men!" shouts Manasseh. "Would ye attack a man fifty to one?"

Blows fall faster and breath comes in short gasps.

The Moslem's horse gives way beneath him, and falls with a shriek backwards. The gallant youth springs to his feet, then throws up his arms and falls. His turban drops off from his brow, and, for the first time, Manasseh recognizes Kedar.

He turns sick. Is the Moslem dead? No, his heart still beats. "Here, men, take him into that house. I will seek him later."

On goes the young leader to a fresh scene of battle. Alas! in the meantime the poorly armed Jews have been everywhere driven back. The Moslems have entered the citadel; the Jews give way before them everywhere. Even his own hopeful spirit cannot revive them. They are seized with a panic and fly, leaving the brave youth almost alone.

Manasseh was soon overpowered, bound, and thrown into the corner of a great hall of the citadel, where he lay apparently forgotten, listening, with heavy heart, to the shrieks and cries of his countrymen without, and to the hum of war, gradually growing fainter, until it ceased, and he knew that the conflict was over. The Moslems began to enter the hall, among them Mohammed.

The prophet took his seat at the end of the apartment, and presently several of the chief citizens were brought in with hands bound. Manasseh perceived that a tribunal was being held, and, from his corner, listened eagerly to the sentence passed upon each.

It soon appeared that treasure was the prophet's aim. Exorbitant demands were made upon the rich merchants, who, pale and trembling, offered their all in exchange for their lives. Among the rest, Kenana, with his handsome wife, was brought in.

"They tell me, Kenana," said the prophet, "that you have immense wealth stored up in this citadel. If you desire your life, inform me where this treasure is."

"I have no treasure in the citadel," said Kenana, proudly; "and if I had, the apostle of Azazil should not know of it."

The prophet's face colored with passion. "Apostle of Azazil! O blasphemer!" he exclaimed. "Do you then thus defy the only, the true prophet of Allah?"

"I do."

"Then we shall see what can be done with a stubborn infidel spirit!" returned Mohammed. "Hither! Apply the torture!"

A machine of fiendish invention was applied to the chief's hands. His fingers were squeezed until the bones cracked; his veins swelled in agony; yet no sound escaped his lips. He could not, or would not, tell where the treasure was concealed, and he was handed over to a Moslem whose brother Kenana had slain. Manasseh closed his eyes in horror, for he knew that Kenana's fate was sealed.

Kenana's wife, Safiya, was taken by Mohammed, and on the homeward march she became the wife of the prophet.

Manasseh lay there in great depression of spirit. He was weary in mind and cramped in body, and it almost seemed as though he were completely forsaken. Yet his ever-present source of comfort returned to him, and like a sweet refrain came the words into his mind: "Thou hast been a strength to the poor, a strength to the needy in his distress, a refuge from the storm, a shadow from the heat, when the blast of the terrible ones is as a storm against the wall."

The half starved Moslem troops now began to clamor for food, and the defenceless Jewish women were forced to prepare victuals and to serve their conquerors. Among these women entered Zaynab, the niece of Asru. She placed a shoulder of mutton before the prophet, then went towards the door. Perceiving Manasseh in the corner, she severed his bonds with a quick stroke of a small dagger, then, shielding him as best she might, she bade him begone.

"Have hope!" she whispered in his ear. "I have poisoned the prophet."

Manasseh uttered an exclamation of horror.

"Why not?" she said, with a laugh. "Manasseh fights with a lance, Zaynab with poison. Now, fly, ere they see you!"

Manasseh hastened down the dark streets to the house in which Kedar had been placed. He found the youth moaning feebly. Hurrying out, he caught a couple of stray camels, and fastened a shugduf in its place. Then, raising the youth in his strong arms, he laid him in the shugduf, and set off in the darkness.

To Mecca he must go. It was a long, weary way. He had little

money, and the few provisions which a Jewish woman in the house gave him would not last long; yet he trusted to Providence, and remembered with satisfaction that the dates were now at their ripest. He would nurse Kedar tenderly; they would journey in the cool shades of night when there was less danger of being stopped on the way. Planning thus, he proceeded, as noiselessly as possible, with his precious burden, through a gap in the wall, and urged his faithful beasts on in the cool night breezes over the blackened plain.

Then he thought of Asru. Asru must not be left to be rudely thrown into a grave by infidel hands. There was danger in it, but he must go back. Kedar was sleeping. He fixed the camels by a charred palm grove, and went back, with flying feet, through the gloom. The towers of Al Kamus rose above him, with lights twinkling on the battlements. He wondered if the prophet were yet alive and what would be the result to Arabia if he were dead. On, on, through the darkness, until the fatal breach was reached. It was quite deserted, peopled only by a heap of dead bodies, from which, in the night time, the superstitious Arabs shrank in horror. Groping among them, he soon came upon Asru's huge form, which he readily recognized by its armor. He dragged the precious clay of his friend from the mass of dead and brought it, with difficulty, outside of the wall; and there beneath a palm tree, he hollowed out a lonely grave, loosening the clay with a battle-axe taken from a dead Arab, and throwing the clods out with his shield. He then cut a wisp of hair from the dead soldier's long locks, placed it in his bosom, kissed the cold brow, and uttered a short prayer over the lifeless form. Tenderly he placed the body in the shallow grave, and covered it with the clay, then, breathing a last farewell, left Asru forever in this life.

In the meantime Mohammed and one of his followers had begun to eat of the poisoned mutton. The soldier was ravenous with hunger, and set upon the tempting roast with eager relish. Mohammed partook of it more slowly.

Suddenly the soldier threw up his arms, and fell back in a convulsion. Mohammed started back in consternation. He, too, felt pain, and raised the cry of "Poison!" The Moslems came rushing in in great alarm. Antidotes were given him, and he shortly recovered, with but a slight sensation of burning in his head. The poor soldier was soon stiff in death.

Mohammed sent for the woman who had brought him the mutton. She came at once.

"Know you who put the poison in this meat?" he asked.

"It was I," she confessed, boldly.

"And how dared you perpetrate so wicked a scheme?"

"If you were a true prophet," she replied, "you would have known that the meat was poisoned; if not, it were a favor to Arabia to rid it of such a despot."

"See then," exclaimed the prophet, "how Allah hath preserved the life of his apostle! Behold, I forgive you. Return to your tribe, and sin not in like manner again."

So saying, with one of his strange freaks of magnanimity, he waved her off, and soon afterward went to rest.

CHAPTER XXV.

MANASSEH AND KEDAR AT MECCA.

"Home, sweet home."

The flame of a smoky oil-dip dimly lighted a spacious room in the house of Amzi. At the low table sat Yusuf and his friend with a chart before them, anxiously following, with eye and finger, the course of Mohammed's northern exploits.

The thoughts of both were with Manasseh. A knock sounded at the bolted door. Yusuf opened it, and there, like a cameo in the setting of darkness, was the youth himself.

"Manasseh, my son!" cried both in astonishment.

He stepped in, now laughing, now brushing tears from his eyes. "There!" he said, freeing himself from their embraces, "I have one more surprise. I come like a grandee, bearing my company in a litter. Help me bring him in."

They stepped out, and Manasseh's second face, that of Kedar, peered from the curtains of the shugduf. None the less warm was the greeting extended to the Moslem, whose weak and trembling frame was an instant call upon their sympathy.

"Now," said Manasseh, piling up a heap of cushions, in his impetuous way, "get us some supper, will you not? I can eat my own share, and half of Kedar's. Like the birds, he takes but a peck at a time."

Supper was ordered, and soon attendants entered bearing platters, until the copper table was burdened with the most tempting dishes of Mecca—roast of spiced lamb, slices of juicy melon and cucumber, pyramids of rice, pomegranates, grapes of Tayf, sweetmeats, fragrant draughts of coffee.

Kedar watched with a languid smile. The peace of this quiet home life affected him almost to tears. Strange had been his emotions when he awoke to consciousness in the shugduf, alone with Manasseh, in the wilderness—feelings first of indignation, then of gratitude, then of admiration for Manasseh, in whom he now discovered the leader of the Jewish horse. And on the way this admiration had ripened into love for the unselfish Jewish youth.

The weariness of the long journey began to tell upon him now, and he was glad that he was among friends. He could eat but little, and was content to listen to Manasseh's bright talk, and to watch him as, with flashing eye and eloquent gesture, he fought over again the Battle of Khaïbar, or when, with hushed tone and tearful eye, he told of the death of Asru, and his lonely burial.

"I must seek his widow and his children," said he. "This is all I have brought them;" and he drew the tangled, bloodstained lock of hair from his bosom.

Silence fell on the little group as they looked upon it, then Yusuf's tones, falling like the low, deep cadence of a chant, repeated the words:

"And there shall be no more curse, but the throne of God and of the Lamb shall be in it; and his servants shall serve him. And they shall see his face; and his name shall be in their foreheads. And there shall be no night there; and they need no candle, neither light of the sun; for the Lord God giveth them light; and they shall reign forever and forever."

"Amen!" responded Amzi, fervently. And Manasseh looked out of the window towards the bright heavens above Abu Kubays, imagining that he could see Asru, clad in shining apparel, with a happy smile on his lips, and the courageous eyes of old looking forth with a new love-light from his radiant countenance.

"Do you know his family?" he asked.

"Ah, yes; they are now regular attendants at the Christian church. They have destroyed all their household gods."

"What!" exclaimed Manasseh, "is this true! How I wish Asru had known it! What joy it would have given him!"

Amzi smiled. "Dare you think, Manasseh, that he does not know it long ere this,—that he did not know it even at the breach of Khaïbar? I like to think that our Asru now has a spiritual body wholly independent of time or space, capable of transporting itself whenever and wherever the mind dictates."

"We cannot know these things as they are, in this time," remarked Yusuf. "But the day is not very far distant now, Amzi, when you and I shall explore these mysteries for ourselves."

So the talk went on. Kedar listened with interest. He thought it a curious conversation, and felt so strangely out of place that it seemed as though he were dreaming, and listening to the talk of genii.

Next morning he was in a decided fever. Then came long days of pain and nights of delirium, in which Manasseh and his two friends hovered like ministering spirits about the youth, whose wounds had healed only to give place to disease far more deadly. In those terrible nights of burning heat his parched tongue swelled so that he could scarcely swallow; he tossed in agony, now fancying himself chained to a rock unable to move, while the prophet urged him on to the heights above where the battle was raging; now imagining himself fastened near a burning furnace whose flames were fed by the bodies of those whom he had slain. He would cry out in terror, and beads of perspiration would start upon his forehead. He lived the whole war over again, and his only rest was at times when, partially conscious, he felt kindly hands placing cool bandages on his burning head, or gently fanning his face.

The time at last came when he sank into a heavy sleep, and awoke calling "Mother."

It was Manasseh who came, almost startled by the naturalness of the tone.

"I have been very ill, Manasseh?"

"Very."

"Long?"

"For weeks. But you must not talk. You will soon be well now."

The invalid closed his eyes, not to sleep, but to think. Presently he opened them.

"Manasseh, if I had died, would I have seen Asru?"

Manasseh was embarrassed. "I—I cannot say," he stammered. "I do not know you well enough to be sure."

"You do not think I should. I do not think so either," he returned decidedly, and closed his eyes again.

In a few days he was able to talk.

"Manasseh, did I hear Yusuf praying for me once when I was ill?"

"He prayed for you every day,—not only that you might be spared to us, but that you might come to know Jesus, and to reject Mohammed."

"I do not think that I ever accepted him—that is, in a religious sense," he returned.

Manasseh's eyes opened wide in astonishment. "Then why did you follow him?" he asked.

"Because, I suppose, his successes dazzled me. It seemed a grand thing to be a hero in the war—to ride, and charge, and drive all before me. Aye, Manasseh, it is after the war that the scales fall from one's eyes."

"How could you, then, follow one whom you did not accept, and must, therefore, have deemed an impostor?"

"I tell you, Manasseh, I gave little heed to matters of religion. For the first time, during the last few days, I have thought of a religious life, or of a hereafter, as I lay here feeling that but for you and your friends, I should even now be in the unknown land beyond the grave."

Manasseh talked long and earnestly to the now convalescent youth. Yusuf and Amzi too talked gently to him when he seemed inclined to hear, but, in his present weak state, they deemed that the consciousness of living in a godly house would appeal more strongly than words of theirs. The weeks passed on, yet he gave no indication that their hopes were being realized. Once indeed he said:

"Manasseh, would that I had had a godly training such as yours!"

"Did your mother not tell you of these things?"

Kedar shook his head. "My poor mother drifted away from her early training in our half heathen Bedouin atmosphere," he said. "The Bedouins know little of Christ. They have traditions of the creation, of the deluge, and such oldtime stories; in all else they are almost heathen. When I am well, Manasseh, we will go to them—to my father—and you will tell them, Manasseh?"

Manasseh nodded a smiling assent.

It was with no little trepidation that Yusuf and Amzi watched for some sign of spiritual growth in the young Bedouin. As the days wore on, and he was able to get about, though still weak, he was willing to attend the Christian meetings; but he sat in silence, and persisted in wearing the garb of a Moslem. The friends did not understand his attitude. They did not recognize the sort of petulant shamefacedness that hindered him from coming forth boldly in defence of principles which he fully endorsed in his secret heart, and made him fear to cut himself loose from the side on which he had taken so bold a stand, lest the epithet of "turn-coat," be fixed upon him. Kedar had not yet been touched by that "live coal" which alone can set man in touch with God, and free him from all human restrictions. But though he said little, he was thinking deeply. He was not indifferent; and there is ever great room for hope where there is not indifference.

And while the little Meccan household was thus engrossed in its own circle, momentous events were happening without the capital.

CHAPTER XXVI.

INTERVENING EVENTS.

During the months that followed, Mohammed still went on in his career of conquest—a course rendered easier day by day, as his enemies were now weak indeed. The tribes of Watiba, Selalima and Bedr speedily gave way before him, but were permitted to remain in their homes upon the payment of a heavy yearly tribute.

He made one more pilgrimage to Mecca, and on this occasion the Koreish, in accordance with the truce, offered no resistance; hence for three days the prophet and his shaven followers walked the streets of Mecca, and performed Tawaf at the Temple.

Mohammed found the Caaba still desecrated by idols, and, while pressing his lips to the sacred Black Stone, he solemnly vowed to conquer Mecca and to remove the pollution of images from the floor of the sanctuary.

In the meantime, the prophet enticed many of the most prominent families of Mecca to his standard. By his marriage with the aunt of Khaled Ibn Waled he secured the alliance of that famous soldier; and by marrying Omm Habiba, daughter of Abu Sofian, he hoped to gain the friendship of his ancient and inveterate enemy.

But time seemed to lag, and his restless spirit soon set itself to look about for some pretext by which he might attack Mecca. A casual skirmish of a few soldiers of the Koreish with a detachment of his soldiers gave the necessary excuse, and he at once charged the Koreish with having broken the truce. They were anxious to make overtures of peace, but Mohammed would listen to nothing.

All saw plainly that no concessions would conciliate a conqueror thus bent upon hostility, and the attitude of Mecca became that of a patient waiting, a dread looking for a surely impending calamity ready to fall at any hour.

And yet, when it did come, the Meccans were not expecting it, so silent, so sudden was the swoop of the conqueror. Every road leading to Mecca was barred by Mohammed, so that none might tell of his plans. All his allies received a mysterious summons to meet him at a point some distance from Mecca, and they came none the less readily that they did not know why they were thus assembled.

With a host of ten thousand men, Mohammed set out over the barren plains, and through the defiles of the mountains. Like a

vast funeral procession the long train wound its way in a silence
broken only by the dull tread of the beasts and the whispered ejac-
ulations of the soldiers. In the night they reached the appointed
valley. Lines of men came pouring in from every side, and at last,
as a signal to all the rest, Omar, the chief in command, gave the
order that the watchfires be lighted,—and at once every summit
sent up its spire of flame.

The citizens of Mecca were stricken with awe.

"I myself will go and see what this means," said Abu Sofian;
and with a single companion he set out over the hills. As they
stood in sight of the great host below, the step of men sounded
near them. They were seized as spies, and hurried off to the tent of
Omar.

The bright light of Omar's campfire revealed the white hair
and flashing eye of the grim old warrior.

"By the prophet of Allah! Ye have brought in a rich prize!"
exclaimed Omar, and his dagger flashed in the firelight as he drew
it to plunge into Abu Sofian's bosom. But deliverance was near.
Out from the darkness galloped Al Abbas, uncle of Mohammed,
mounted on the prophet's white mule. He caught the Meccan up
with him, and hastened off to the tent of the prophet.

"Ha!" exclaimed Mohammed, "you have come at last, Abu
Sofian, to acknowledge the supremacy of the prophet of Allah?"

"I come," said Abu Sofian surlily, "to beg mercy for my
people."

"Will you, then, acknowledge Mohammed as the prophet of
God? Do this, Abu Sofian, and thy life shall be spared, and terms
of peace granted to all Meccans who are willing to follow their
leader's example."

Abu Sofian gave a surly assent, and was set free. Favorable
terms for the inhabitants of the city were then presented to him;
and, that he might be able to take back with him a full account of
the strength of the prophet's army, he was placed with Al Abbas at
the head of a narrow defile, through which the whole army, with
fluttering banners and proudly flapping standards, passed before
him.

Even the stern old warrior stood aghast at the mighty multitude. He returned to the city, and, from the roof of the Caaba,
once more assembled the people of Mecca. Then, while they listened, with bowed heads and heaving sobs, he told them of the
great host, of the uselessness of resistance, and of the terms
offered in case of submission. To this course, humiliating as it was,
he strongly urged them. Silent in despair, or weeping wildly, they

returned to their homes, and that night the darkness which fell seemed like a pall upon the stricken city.

CHAPTER XXVII.

THE TRIUMPHANT ENTRANCE INTO MECCA.

"One murder made a villain; millions, a hero."—Porteus.

Upon the following morning ere the sun rose, a deputation was sent to the prophet to inform him that his terms had been accepted.

The people of Mecca were curious to note the triumphant entrance of the great conqueror. Many, indeed, threw themselves upon their faces in agony of lost hope; but the housetops swarmed with people, and the side of Abu Kubays was moving with a dense crowd of women and children, who, at a safe distance, watched for the strange pageant.

The prophet was allowed to enter the borders of the town unmolested, but when the deserter, Khaled Ibn Waled, appeared, the rage of the Koreish knew no bounds; a howl of derision arose, and an ungovernable mob fired straight upon him with their arrows. Khaled dashed upon them with sword and lance, but Mohammed, noting the commotion, rode up and ordered him to desist.

The mêlée subsided, and, just as the sun rose over Abu Kubays, the conqueror entered the city. He was habited in scarlet, and mounted upon a large Syrian camel; and, as he rode, followed by the whole host of his army, he repeated aloud passages from the Koran.

Straight on towards the Caaba he went, looking neither to right nor to left. Its gates were thrown open before him, and the vast procession, with the prophet at its head, performed Tawaf about the temple. Then, ere the mighty trampling ceased, Mohammed entered the Caaba—that Caaba in which he had been spat upon and covered with mud thrown by derisive hands. Little wonder that he felt his triumph complete!

Three hundred and sixty idols still stared from the walls of the temple, and, ere night fell, not an image remained to pollute an edifice in which, if in ever so blind a manner, the name of the living God had been once mentioned.

Mohammed then took his stand upon the little hill Al Safa, and gave the command that every man, woman, and child in Mecca, save those detained by illness, should pass before him.

Kedar found his weakness a sufficient reason for remaining at home, but Yusuf, Amzi, and Manasseh were forced to join the long procession.

One by one, the inhabitants knelt before the victor, renouncing idolatry and declaring their fealty to him as their governor and spiritual head. But a few among the Christian Jews refused to acknowledge him as the prophet of God.

"As conqueror we accept you," they said; "as subjects we will obey you in all that does not interfere with our worship of the true God, and his Son, the Christ. But as Mohammed prophet of God, we will not acknowledge you."

The prophet, however, was in a lenient frame of mind. At no time a cruel tyrant when victory was once assured, he was still less inclined to be so upon a day when everything augured so favorably for the future. Moreover, when it seemed to him practicable, Mohammed delighted in showing mercy. This trait is but one of the incomprehensible features of his strange, contradictory character.

"So be it," he returned, graciously. "I give you your lives and property. They are a gift from the prophet ye despise. Yet, lest ye be stirrers up of sedition, I enjoin you to leave the city with what expedition ye will. Go where ye please, provided it be out of my dominions; take what time ye need to settle your affairs, and dispose of your property; then, in the name of Allah, I bid you good speed."

The Jews, among them Yusuf and Amzi, passed thankfully on. A tall, gaunt, Bedouin woman, with flashing eyes and hands showing like the claws of a vulture beneath her black robe, came next. It was Henda in disguise.

"What!" exclaimed the prophet, with a smile, "has Abu Sofian taken to the hills again, that his wife thus comes in Bedouin garb?"

Henda, seeing that her disguise was penetrated, fell at his feet imploring for pardon.

"I forgive you freely," he said, raising her to her feet. "You will now acknowledge your prophet?"

"Never!" cried the Koreish woman.

"Boldly said!" returned Mohammed. "The wife of Abu Sofian doth not readily follow in the path of her master. He has trained her but poorly. Yet, go in peace, O daughter of the Koreish, and know that the prophet of Islam has a merciful heart."

Thus passed the whole long day until the stars shone through the blue; and Mohammed went to rest, serene in his triumph, yet troubled by bodily pain, for, ever since he had eaten the poisoned mutton at Khaïbar, his health had been steadily declining.

In a few days he returned to Medina. A fresh revelation of the Koran, commending fully his doctrine of the sword, was there proclaimed from the mosque; and to Khaled was given the task of subjugating the remaining tribes.

The prophet's health now began to give way rapidly, and he resolved upon a last pilgrimage to the holy city. In the month Ramadhan, at the head of one hundred thousand men, the mightiest expedition he had ever led, he started for Mecca. He rode in a litter, and about him were his nine wives, also seated in litters; while, at the rear of the procession, trudged a great array of camels destined for sacrifice, and gayly decorated with ribbons and flowers.

About a day's journey from Mecca, at twilight, the vast host met the troops of Ali, returning from an expedition into Yemen, and these immediately turned with the pilgrimage. It was a weird and impressive scene. In the night, the augmented host now pressed onward, with increased impatience, over a plain strewn with basaltic drift. The soft thud of padded feet sounded over the hard ground. Huge camels loomed shapelessly through the uncertain haze. No voice of mirth or singing arose from the vast assemblage, but the night-wind sighed through the ribs of the scant-leaved acacias above, and stooped to blow the red flames of the torches back in a smoky glare; while, here and there, a more pretentious light, issuing from between the curtains of a shugduf, shed a passing gleam upon the dusky faces of the pilgrims, plodding like eerie genii of the night over the barren wilds.

Next morning, the host reached Mecca. The prophet once more entered the sacred courtyard of the temple, and was borne sadly about the Caaba in Tawaf. Then, weak as he was, he insisted upon taking part in the sacrificial ceremony. With his own hand he slew sixty-three camels, one for each year of his life. Then he ascended the pulpit and preached to the people.

Upon his return to Medina, he preached again from the mosque, enjoining upon the faithful strict compliance with the form of worship set forth in the Koran and by the example of the prophet—the giving of alms; prayer towards the kebla; the performance of Tawaf, and ablutions at Zem-Zem; prostration prayers at the Caaba, and all the rites of pilgrimage. Thus did Mohammed formulate the rules for the future guidance of the Moslem world.

CHAPTER XXVIII.

KEDAR AT THE CAABA.

Once more the shades of night hung over the Eastern world. And there, while the hush of slumber fell upon the hills of the North, the cities of the South awoke to life and bustle, for during the earlier half of the hours of darkness the Oriental awakes from the lethargy of the day, and really begins to live. The moon, almost at full, and glowing like a silver orb on a purple sea, rose slowly over the black top of Abu Kubays, tipping its crest with a shimmering line of light, and throwing its radiance across the vale below, where all lay shapeless in shade save the top of the huge temple, which, with its pall-like kiswah (curtain), arose like a bier above the low houses about it. Upon it the moonbeams fell with solemn, white light, and the young man standing alone by one of the pillars of the portico felt a thrill of awe as he looked upon the mysterious structure, and thought of the great antiquity of the institution.

For the moment, lost in contemplation, he was oblivious to the swarming of the dusky multitudes now pouring into the courtyard on all sides. Then, as the increasing hum fell upon his ears, he gave them his attention. It was the scene of which he had so often heard, and upon which he now looked for the first time. There were the people at Tawaf, walking, running, or standing with upturned eyes, sanctimoniously repeating passages of the Koran; there were the frantic few clinging to the great folds of the kiswah, as though its contact procured for them eternal salvation; there were the crowds gulping down copious draughts of the brackish water of Zem-Zem, or pouring it upon their heads.

There, too, within a stone's throw of the temple, were the busy stalls of the venders, whence issued cries of:

"Cucumbers! Cucumbers O!"

"Grapes! Grapes!—luscious and juicy with the crystal dews of Tayf! Grapes, O faithful!"

"Who will buy cloth of Damascus, rich and fit for a king? Come, buy thy lady a veil! Buy a veil to screen her charms blooming as the rosy light of morn, to screen her hair black as midnight shades on the hills of Nejd, and her eyes sparkling like diamonds of Oman!"

"O water! Precious water from Zem-Zem! Water to wash away thy sin, and help thee into Paradise! O believer, buy water of Zem-

Zem!"

And there, beneath the twinkling lights of the portico, sat a group of Abyssinian girls, waiting to be sold as slaves.

As the youth looked upon it all with no little curiosity he observed the crowd give way before a man clothed wholly in white, who proceeded directly to the Caaba and, pausing beneath the door, gave utterance to a loud prayer, while the people about fell prostrate on the ground. Then, in a loud voice, he commanded that the stair be brought. Attendants hastened to roll the bulky structure into its place, and the priest, or guardian of the temple, ascended, and received from his attendants several buckets of water which he carried into the edifice.

Presently, small streams began to trickle from the doorway, and the guardian's white vestments again appeared, as he proceeded to sweep the water out, dashing it far over the steps. The people rushed beneath it, crowding over one another in their anxiety holding their upturned faces towards it and counting themselves blessed if a drop of it fell upon them. It was the ceremony of washing the Caaba.

The youth beside the pillar, though he wore Moslem garb, looked on in contempt; and, barely waiting for the conclusion of the ceremony, walked proudly from the enclosure, merely pausing to examine somewhat critically the Black Stone, which, deserted for the moment, was visible in the red light of a torch above. Then, passing through the nearest gate, he walked, rather feebly, towards the house of Amzi.

Yusuf, wearied after a long day's work, was resting upon the carpeted Mastabah (platform) which forms a part of the vestibule of every comfortable house in Mecca. There was no light in the apartment save that afforded by the dim glimmer of a fire-pan, over which bubbled a fragrant urn of coffee. His thoughts had been wandering back over the events of his changeful life; events which would culminate, as far as his immediate history was concerned, in his early banishment from this city of his adoption. The little Jewish band would go together—precisely where, they did not know,—Amzi, Manasseh, the family of Asru, a few other devoted souls, and, it was to be hoped, Kedar.

Yusuf's thoughts dwelt upon Kedar. Tonight he seemed to feel a sweet assurance that his prayers in the youth's behalf were soon to be answered; and, in the darkness, he cried out for the lad's salvation, until the blessed Lord seemed so near that he almost fancied he could put forth his hand and feel the strong, loving, helping touch of Him who said, "I am the good shepherd, and know my sheep, and am known of mine . . . . And other sheep I have, which are not of this fold; them also I must bring; and they shall hear my voice; and there shall be one fold, and one shepherd."

A step sounded on the doorstone, and the very youth of whom Yusuf was thinking entered.

"Well, my Kedar," said the priest, "have you been enjoying the moon?"

"I have been to the Caaba," returned Kedar, with amused contempt in his voice, "yet I have neither swung by the kiswah nor drenched myself, like a rain-draggled hen, at Zem-Zem."

"And you have not kissed the Black Stone?"

"Neither have I kissed the stone. By my faith, if it has become blackened by the kiss of sinners, those poor simpletons caress it in vain! On the word of a Bedouin, it can hold no more, since it is as black as well may be already."

"The worship of our little church, then, suits you better?" The priest's tone scarcely concealed the anxiety with which he asked the question.

"You seem to worship in truth," returned the youth, solemnly. "You seem to find a comfort in your service which these poor blindlings seek in vain. Aye, Yusuf, in living among you I have noted the peaceful tenor of your lives, the rest and confidence which nothing seems to overthrow. You rejoice in life, yet you do not fear death! Could such a life be mine, I would gladly accept it. But I do not seem to be one of you."

The priest made no reply for a moment. Kedar did not know that he was praying for the fit word. Then his deep, tender tones broke the silence.

"You believe in Jesus, whom we love?"

"I believe that he was the Son of God; that he lived on the very hills to the north of us; that he died to reveal to us the greatness of his love. Yet—" He paused.

"'Whosoever believeth on the Son hath everlasting life,'" said Yusuf in a low tone.

"I know, but—" the youth hesitated again.

"But what, Kedar?" asked the priest.

"Jesus said to Nicodemus," returned the youth, "'Except a man be born again, he cannot see the kingdom of heaven.' Yusuf, this is what bothers me. I cannot understand this being born again."

"Let us call it, then, just 'beginning to love and trust Jesus,'" said Yusuf quietly.

Kedar almost started in his surprise. This aspect of the question had never appeared to him before. For a long time he sat, deep in thought, and Yusuf did not break in upon his meditations.

"Is that all?" he asked at length.

"That is all," returned Yusuf. "To trust him you must believe in him, love him, recognize his love, and leave everything to his guidance—everything in this physical life, in your spiritual life, and in the life to come. Then you will find peace. All your days will be spent in a loving round of happy labor, in which no work seems low or trifling—happy because love to Jesus begets the wish to do his will in every affair of life; and perfect love renders service, not a bondage, but the joyful spontaneity of freedom."

Kedar was again silent, then he said slowly:

"Yusuf, I begin to understand it all now; yet—is there something wrong still?—I have not the overpowering thrill of joy, the exuberance of feeling, the wondrous rapture of delight, which Amzi says he experienced, when, in the prison of Medina, he saw the light."

"Be not discouraged, my son," was the reply. "To different temperaments, in religion as in all else, the truth appeals in different ways. If you are trusting implicitly now in God's love, go on without doubt or fear. Most Christians—growing Christians—find that at different stages in their experience certain truths stand out more clearly, and, as the days go by, their difficulties clear away like mists before the morning sun."

"Yusuf, can I ever become such a Christian as you?" returned Kedar, in a half awed tone at the thought.

"My son, look not on me," returned Yusuf, tenderly. "Strive only to perceive Jesus in all your life, to find him a reality to you—a companion, ever with you, walking by your side in the hot mart, riding by you in the desert, sitting by you in solitude,—then, where he is, evil cannot come. Your life will become all upright, conscientious, and loving, for his life will show through yours."

"And do temptations never come to those so blessed?"

"Ah, yes, Kedar, so long as life lasts 'our adversary, the devil, goeth about as a roaring lion, seeking whom he may devour.' Yet, think you that the God who 'stretcheth out the heavens as a curtain, who layeth the beams of his chambers in the waters, who maketh the clouds his chariot, who walketh upon the wings of the wind, who maketh his angels spirits, his ministers a naming fire'—think you that such an One is not able to stand between you and the tempter? Think you that he before whom devils cried out in fear, is not able to deliver you from the power of evil? Kedar, know that the Christian may even glory in his own weakness, for Jesus has said, 'My strength is made perfect in weakness;' and yet, while thus feeling his helplessness, the believer must ever be conscious of the unconquerable strength of Christ, and should rest serene in the knowledge that, clothed in the full armor of God, he is able to withstand all the darts of the wicked one."

Kedar said no more, but from that hour his humility, his patience, his gentleness, began to show forth as the outcome of the power of that working of the Spirit, whose fruit is "love, joy, peace, long-suffering, gentleness, goodness, faith, meekness, temperance."

CHAPTER XXIX.

KEDAR RETURNS TO HIS HOME.

*"Death exempts not a man from being, but only presents an
alteration."*
—Bacon.

When Kedar left Yusuf on that memorable night it was not to
sleep. He ascended the stair and went out upon the hanging balcony, where he could look at the sky and the mountains, and
ponder over the conversation of the evening. His was not the
excitable, rapturous joy experienced by many, but a feeling of
quiet contentment that settled upon his soul, and brought a calm
smile to his features.

So he sat, when Manasseh burst upon him exclaiming,
"What! my invalid able to stay up all the night as well as half the
day! Come, listen to me! I have news!"

"Yes?"

"This evening a courier from Medina arrived in the city. He
has with him a proclamation requiring all unsubmissive Jews to
leave Mecca by tomorrow night at the latest."

"So soon!" exclaimed Kedar. "Where are they to go?"

"I have just talked with Yusuf, and with Amzi, who, poor fat
man! is trying to get a little sleep in the fresh air of the housetop.
They propose that we join my father's family in Palestine. Of
course, I do not object!" added the youth, with a smile.

"Think you it will be safe for so small a band to face the dangers of the desert alone?" asked Kedar.

"A caravan leaves for Damascus tomorrow," replied
Manasseh. "Fortunately we may obtain its protection."

"Good! Then I shall turn aside to the tablelands of Nejd and
see my parents again," said Kedar.

"Think you your parents would join our band?"

Kedar shook his head. "Not likely. You see my father has lived
all his days as a Bedouin. To be tied down to commerce he would
consider a degradation. Neither would he become a shepherd, as
watching sheep is a task held fit for women only in our tribe."

"And will you stay with them, Kedar?" asked Manasseh.

"I know not. We will see what the future has in store; but, at
any rate," he added, half slyly, "your cousin Kedar will wear the
Moslem turban no more."

The tone, rather than the words, told all. Manasseh took a quick, sharp look at the face smiling quietly in the moonlight, then he seized Kedar's hand warmly and whispered, "I am glad."

The following day was spent in packing and bidding adieux. Yusuf and Amzi passed the last hours among their poor, and, from the housetop, Kedar and Manasseh saw them returning in the evening, followed by a ragged crowd who clung to their gowns or wiped tearful eyes with tattered sleeves.

The sun went down as the caravan left the city, and on an eminence above, the little Jewish band stopped to take a last look at their old home—Mecca, with its low houses, its crooked streets, its mystic Caaba, and its weird mountain scenery.

All gray it lay beneath the shades of falling night; yet, as they looked, a wondrous change ensued. Gradually the landscape began to brighten; the houses shone forth; the aloe trees became green; the side of Abu Kubays sparkled with a seemingly self-emitted light; the rocks of the red mountain were dyed with a rosy glow; the Caaba grew more and more distinct, until even the folds of its kiswah were visible; and the sand of the narrow valley shone, beneath a saffron sky above, with a coppery radiance. It was the wondrous "afterglow" of the Orient,—a scene unique in its beauty, yet not often beheld in so sheltered a spot as Mecca.

The exiles, with tearful eyes, looked upon the fair landscape, which thus seemed to bid them an inanimate farewell. Then, as the glow paled and the rocks again took their sombre hue, and the city faded in redoubled shadow, the little band turned slowly away, and followed in the wake of the caravan now winding through the pass at some distance.

The Hebrew band consisted of twenty souls, among whom were Sherah, the daughter of Asru, and her mother, and the old white-haired man Benjamin, who had preached in the church and had become a father indeed to Asru's family.

Needless to speak of the long, tedious journey. Suffice it to say that, while the caravan wound through the north of El Hejaz, Kedar and Manasseh turned aside to the fresher plateaux of the Nejd, and the Bedouin once more found himself amid the scenes of his boyhood.

His spirits rose as the cool breeze from the plains struck him. The vision of sweet home—sweet to the roving Bedouin as to the pampered child of luxury—rose before him, and he urged his horse on with an ever-increasing anxiety.

From neighboring tribes they found out the way to Musa's present encampment, then, spurring their horses on over a crisp plain, and beguiling the time with many a laugh and jest, they proceeded in the direction indicated, until, in a broad valley, the circle of tents lay before them.

"Come, Manasseh," said Kedar, "let us give them a surprise. Let us take a turn up yonder hill and swoop down upon them like a falcon."

"Agreed!" quoth Manasseh; and, with almost childish pleasure, they proceeded to make a short detour, and then galloped rapidly down from the hill-crest.

The encampment was strangely quiet.

"What is the matter, Manasseh?" asked Kedar. "There is scarcely anyone about."

A few dogs now set up a savage barking, and a man came out with a heavy whip and drove them, yelping, away.

"What is wrong, Tema?" asked Kedar, anxiously.

"Alas, my young master," said the man, "your father will soon be no more."

The youth sprang to the ground and entered the chief's tent. There lay the brave old Sheikh, dying, as he had scorned to die, in his bed, with pallid face and closed eyes, his gray hair damp and tangled, and his grizzled beard descending upon his brawny chest, from which the folds of his garments were drawn back. About him knelt his wife and children. Lois raised a tear-stained face to her son, then buried it again in her hands. Kedar threw himself beside the couch. The old man's lips moved.

"Aha!" cried he, "it is blood-revenge! Mizni, bold chief, I have you now! Yes, fly up to your eyrie among the rocks, if you can. I shall reach you there! Blood must be spilled. My honor! My honor!"

He was thinking of a fray of his youth in which he had paid the dues of blood for an only brother. Again, he seemed to be dashing on in the chase.

"On, on, Zebe!" he cried, in a hoarse whisper, "on, good steed! The quarry is ahead there! See the falcon swoop! Good steed, on!"

His voice was growing fainter, yet he continued to wave his arms feebly, and to move his lips in inaudible muttering. Once more the words became distinct:

"Here, Kedar, little man! Let father put you on his horse. There, boy, there! You will make a son for a Bedouin to be proud of!"

A tear rolled down Kedar's cheek as the dying man thus pictured a happy scene of his childhood. "Poor old father!" he murmured. "Manasseh, it is hard to see him die thus godlessly. Had I but come sooner!"

The old Sheikh's breath came shorter. His hand moved more feebly; he turned his head uneasily and opened his eyes.

He fixed them upon his son with a look of consciousness. His face brightened.

"Dear father," whispered the youth, and kissed his cheek.

A smile spread over the old man's face. His lips formed the words "My son!" His eyes closed, and the old Bedouin was dead.

The women broke into a low wail, and Kedar, with a tenderness not of the old time, strove to comfort his mother. The rites of anointing the body for burial were performed, and all through the evening the different members of the tribe gathered mournfully in to take a last look at the brave old leader.

When night fell Kedar went out; the atmosphere of the tent seemed to choke him. Manasseh stood silently by his side. The wail of the women sounded in a low burial-song from within, and groups of men, talking in whispers, gathered before the door.

Kedar stood with folded arms and head thrown back, looking upon the heavens. A star fell. Every Bedouin bowed his head, for the Arabs believe that when a star falls a soul ascends to paradise.

"Manasseh," said Kedar in a low tone, "I cannot let them bury him. They would do it with half heathen rites."

"Can none among all these conduct Christian service?"

"Not one. My mother is the only one who knows aught of Christianity."

"Then," said Manasseh, "if you will let me, I shall offer prayers above his grave."

"No, Manasseh," said Kedar decidedly, "these people would resent it in a stranger. I shall do it; they will grant me the privilege as the right of a son."

"And rightly," exclaimed Manasseh, surprised and pleased at the staunchness with which his cousin took his new stand.

On the following day the funeral wound slowly up the defile to the place of the lonely grave. And there Kedar prayed simply and earnestly, a prayer in which the spiritual enlightenment of the sorrowful people about him was the chief theme. They did not understand all its meaning, but they were impressed by the solemnity and sincerity of the young Arab's manner.

Then the little heap of sand was raised, and four stone slabs were placed, according to Bedouin custom, upon the grave.

CHAPTER XXX.

THE DEATH OF MOHAMMED.

"Nothing can we call our own but death"—Shakespeare.

While Musa thus lay dying in the tents of Nejd, the cold hand of death was fast closing upon another in the land of Arabia. Day by day the germs of disease pulsed stronger and stronger through the veins of Mohammed. Monarch of Arabia, originator of a creed which was eventually to push itself throughout Egypt, India, Afghanistan, Persia, and even to the wild steppes of Siberia, he must now die. He viewed the end with firmness, and it has been a matter of controversy as to whether in these later days he still had the hallucination of being a prophet.

Too feeble to walk to the mosque, he lay, tended by his wives, in the tent of Ayesha, his favorite. Not many days before his death he asked that he might be carried to the mosque. Willing arms bore him thither, and placed him in the pulpit, from whence he could look down upon the city, and away to the palm groves of Kuba. Then, turning his face towards the holy city, Mecca, he addressed the crowds of waiting people below.

"If there be any man," said he, "whom I have unjustly scourged, I submit my own back to the lash of retaliation. Have I aspersed the reputation of any Mussulman?—let him proclaim my faults in the face of the congregation. Has anyone been despoiled of his goods?—the little that I possess shall compensate the principal and the interest of the debt."

He then liberated his slaves, gave directions as to the order of his funeral, and appointed Abu Beker to supply his place in offering public prayer. This seemed to indicate that Abu Beker was to be his successor in office; and the long-tried friend accordingly became the first caliph of the Saracen empire.

After this the prophet was conveyed again to the house of Ayesha. The fever increased, and the pain in his head became so great that he more than once pressed his hands upon it exclaiming, "The poison of Khaïbar! The poison of Khaïbar!"

Once, perceiving the mother of Bashar, the soldier who had died of the poison in the fatal city, he said:

"O mother of Bashar, the cords of my heart are now breaking of the food which I ate with your son at Khaïbar!"

At another time, springing up in delirium, he called for pen and ink that he might write a new revelation; but owing to his weak state, his request was refused. In talking to those about him he said that Azraël, the Angel of Death, had not dared to take his soul until he had asked his permission.

A few nights before his death, he awoke from a troubled sleep, and, starting wildly from his couch, sprang up with unnatural strength from his bed.

"Come, Belus!" he cried to an attendant. "Come with me to the burial place of El Bakia! The dead call to me from their graves, and I must go thither to pray for them."

Alone they passed into the night; through the long, silent streets they walked like phantoms; up the white road of Nedj they glided, until the few low tombs of the cemetery to the southeast of the city were in sight.

At the border of the bleak, lonely field, where the wind moaned among the tombs like the sighing of a weeping Rachel, Mohammed paused.

"Peace be with you, O people of El Bakia!" he cried. "Peace be with you, martyrs of El Bakia! One and all, peace be with you! We verily, if Allah please, are about to join you! O Allah, pardon us and them! And the mercy of God and his blessings be upon us all!"

Thus he prayed, stretching his hands towards the spot where his friends lay in their long sleep. His companion stood in awe behind him, shivering in superstitious terror, as the white tombs gleamed like moving apparitions through the gloom, and the night-owls hooted with a mournful cadence o'er the dreary waste.

When he had concluded, the prophet turned towards home. But the excitement of mind which had endowed him with almost supernatural strength now deserted him. His steps grew feeble and he was fain to lean upon Belus on his painful way back.

He grew rapidly worse. His wife Ayesha, and his daughter Fatima, wife of Ali, seldom left his bedside. When the last came, he raised his eyes to the ceiling and exclaimed, "O Allah, pardon my sins!" He then, with his own feeble hand, sprinkled his face with water, and soon afterwards, with his head on Ayesha's bosom, he departed, in the sixty-third year of his age, and the eleventh year of the Hejira, A.D. 632.

The frenzied people would not believe that he was dead. "He will arise, like Jesus," they said. But no returning breath quivered through the cold lips or animated the rigid form of him whom they passionately called to life; and not until Abu Beker assured them that he was really no more, saying, "Did he not himself assure us that he must experience the common fate of all? Did he not say in the Koran, 'Mohammed is no more than an apostle; the other apostles have already deceased before him; if he die therefore, or be slain, will ye turn back on your heels?'"—not until then did they disperse, with deep groans.

Mohammed was buried in the house in which he died, his grave being dug in the spot beneath his bed; but some years later a stone tomb was erected over the grave, and until the present day the place is held so sacred that it is at the risk of his life that anyone but a Mussulman dares enter.

CHAPTER XXXI.

THE NEW HOME.

"On these small cares of daughter, wife, or friend,
The almost sacred joys of Home depend."
—Hannah More.

In the quiet valley in Palestine life had been dealing gently with Nathan and his family. The long, long absence of Manasseh was the one thing lacking for their perfect contentment.

"It is well," Nathan would say, yet his eyes would turn wistfully towards the South, as though he half hoped to see the beloved face of his son appearing over the hill. The mother grew weary with waiting, yet she did not murmur, but whispered to her lonely heart, "Living or dead, it must be well." Only once she said, "Husband, he is surely dead," and Nathan replied:

"Let us still hope, wife, that we may yet see the goodness of the Lord in permitting us to behold his face."

So they hoped on, and worked on, amid their orange trees, their corn and vegetables, and their sheep browsing peacefully on the hills. And Mary tended the jasmine flowers and rosebushes at the door, carrying water to them night and morning, that they might look at their prettiest when Manasseh came. Only one letter had reached them—a cheery, hopeful letter,—but it had been a long time on the way, and the events of which it told had taken place many weeks before it reached the Jordan valley. It had told them of Yusuf and Amzi, of the little church, of the sender's strange meeting with Kedar, and the news he had gathered of Lois. Then it had told of the war, and had closed with an affectionate farewell, in which the writer expressed his wish, rather than his expectation, of being able to make his way to the new home soon.

How long it seemed to Mary since that last word had come! And he was not home yet! She kept the precious manuscript in her bosom, and twenty times a day she looked down the long valley for the well-known form. One morning she sat by the river, idly plashing her bare feet in its golden ripples, and looking at the shadows on the little stones near the shore. About her gamboled a pet lamb, and above, a soft blue sky was flecked with fleecy white clouds. She twirled a sprig of blossoms in her hand, but her thoughts were far away in dear, hot, dusty, dreary Mecca.

"It is not so pleasant as this, though," she thought, "if Manasseh were only here."

Just then the tinkle of a camel bell was heard,—a strange sound in that secluded spot. Mary looked up, and saw what seemed to be a great many people coming over the hill, camels bearing shugdufs, too, and packmules, heavily laden.

Trembling, she rushed into the house.

"Oh, mother, what means this? See the people! Manasseh would not bring all of those with him?"

The mother shaded her eyes with her hand, and looked forth, anxiously.

Nearer and nearer came the train. Who were they? Not Manasseh; Manasseh would not come so slowly. Can it be? Not Yusuf! Not Amzi! Yes, yes! O joy! It is they!—and many other familiar faces smile also from the train!

"Is Manasseh well?"

"Yes, Manasseh is well, and happy."

So questions were asked and answered in joyful confusion; and Nathan came in from the hills to bid the travelers welcome. Then the dusty, travel-stained tents were pitched once more, this time on a grassy slope by the rippling Jordan. A simple repast was spread, and the company dined in royal state.

With what surprise did Nathan and his household greet the wife of Asru and her sweet-faced daughter as sisters in Christ, and with what sympathy did they hear of Asru's sad death!

Then plans for the immediate settlement of the little party were made. Pastureland in abundance was to be had; hence the majority of the newcomers would be speedily and comfortably provided with new homes. Amzi would take up his abode in some comfortable townhouse not far distant, and Yusuf would remain with him for the present.

Mary and Sherah were friends at once, and ere evening fell, they sat, as girls will, in a cozy nook by the riverside forming plans for walks and talks during the long, bright, summer days.

Every cloud had drifted, for the time being, from the happy company; and, ere they retired to rest, all united with fervor in the words of the grand song:

"Bless the Lord, O my soul, and forget not all his benefits: who forgiveth all thine iniquities; who healeth all thy diseases; who redeemeth thy life from destruction; who crowneth thee with loving kindness and tender mercies; who satisfieth thy mouth with good things; so that thy youth is renewed like the eagle's. The Lord executeth righteousness and judgment for all that are oppressed . . . . Bless the Lord, all his works, in all places of his dominion! Bless the Lord, O my soul!"

And later in that same evening, another group came to Nathan's house. The door was closed, for the evening was chill without. A knock was heard. Mary opened the door, and there was Manasseh himself, radiantly happy; and close behind him was another Manasseh with Bedouin eyes.

Mother, sister, and father pressed round the youth until he could scarcely move.

"There, there!" he said, shaking them off playfully, "my cousin Kedar will be jealous. Mother, this is Lois' son, and there is someone in the darkness here still."

The youth went out. Who was this that he assisted from the shugduf?—the living image of Lois in her girlhood days! Not Lois, but her daughter, a Bedouin maid, fresh as the breeze from her native hills. And can this be Lois—this sad-faced yet stately woman? It is, indeed, and the long-separated sisters are once more united. Kedar's brothers are there too, and one more family is added to the little community.

CHAPTER XXXII.

A WEDDING IN PALESTINE.

"God, the best maker of all marriages."—Shakespeare.

For a moment let us look more closely at the little district where the Jewish band found a home after all their wanderings.

They settled at a point where the Jordan River, that strange river flowing for its entire length through a depression one thousand feet below the level of the sea, is cut up by many a cataract; and the rushing noise of the water, carried from its mysterious source at the foot of Mount Hermon, fills the valley with a music not lost upon ears long accustomed to the dry wastes of Arabian deserts. To the north lie plains where cold blasts blow, and mountains whose crests gleam with never-failing snow; yet in the fair vales of Jordan the tempered breeze fans the air with the mildness of a never-ceasing summer, and the soft alluvial soil is luxuriant with the rich growth of the tropics. To the west the rugged and picturesque mountains of Judea rise, and to the east, at a distance of some ten miles, lie the blue-tinted mountains of Moab, rich in associations of sacred history.

In this favored spot, shaded by waving groves and hidden by vines, was the house of Asru's wife; and at a little distance from it was a well, an old-fashioned well such as is seen only in the East, walled about with ancient and worn flagstones, between which, at one side, the water trickled and ran over mossy stones to the river below.

A large tamarisk tree waved above it, and in its shade, with one knee resting on the flagstone, her hands clasped behind her head, and her large eyes fixed upon the mountains of Moab beyond, stood Sherah, ere the sun rose, on one beautiful autumn morning.

An earthen water pitcher, such as is carried by the girls of the Orient, was beside her, yet she moved not to execute her errand.

The sun arose behind the mountain; the amber sky became golden; the rosy pink clouds changed to radiant silver; the birds sang; the dew glittered; and the sun shone through the leaves of the trees with a flush of green-gold.

The beauty of the scene touched the girl. In a low, clear voice, spontaneous as the song of a bird, she sang: "For the Lord shall comfort Zion; he will comfort her waste places: and he will make her wilderness like Eden, and her desert like the garden of the Lord; joy and gladness shall be found therein, thanksgiving and the voice of melody."

The song brought comfort to her; for was she not soon to leave this fairy spot, this Aidenn, to return to the land of the Mussulman; not the land of—

> "Deep myrrh thickets blowing round
> The stately cedar, tamarisks.
> Thick rosaries of scented thorn,
> Tall Orient shrubs, and obelisks
> Graven with emblems of the time,"

but to the bleak, treeless plains of Nejd, breezy with the warm breath of desert-swept winds, bounded by rolling mountains, and dotted by the black tents of those roving hordes of whom it has been said that "their hand is against every man, and every man's hand is against them,"—the fierce, cruel yet generous, impulsive, courteous tribes of the desert.

For Manasseh and Kedar were both going back to the desert tribes, braving the dangers of persecution, that they might exert an influence in christianizing the Bedouin tribes over whom the Moslems as yet had little power. Sherah was going back as Manasseh's wife, and this was her wedding day. She was willing to go, yet she could not help feeling a little lonely on this last morning in her mother's home.

Presently the call "Sherah! Sherah!" came through the olive groves, and the old nurse hobbled out. The woman was a thorough type of an aged Arab, lean, wrinkled, hook-nosed, with skin like shrunken leather, and a voice like a raven. Yet Sherah knew her goodness of heart, and loved her dearly. She was taking the old woman back with her, for, oddly enough, Zama had never felt at home in the new land, and often craved that her bones might be buried in the old soil.

"Why disturb me, Zama?" said the young woman kindly. "See you not that I am bidding farewell to this dear valley?"

"Aye, aye, child," muttered the old nurse, "but we must put the wedding-gown upon you, and twine jasmine in your hair." She stroked the glossy masses fondly. "Ah, tomorrow it must be braided in the plaits of the matron, and the coins will be placed about my precious one's neck; yet it seems only yesterday that she was a toddling baby at my feet."

The two women, the one tall and lithe as a willow, the other bent and shrunken, took their way to the house. Mary was already there, and assisted in adorning the bride.

The guests arrived, and the simple ceremony was soon over; then the company sat down to the wedding feast. Lois and her sister talked in low tones to the mother of Sherah, who grieved a little at the separation from her daughter. Happy jests and laughter passed about among the young people. Amzi went, with beaming face, from group to group; and Yusuf looked quietly on.

In the midst of the entertainment some one came to the door.

"It is a peddler!" cried one. "Let us see what he has—perhaps another gift for our fair bride."

The young people gathered about the glittering trinkets. Manasseh came near, and, with a merry twinkle in his eyes, placed his hand on the man's shoulder. The peddler looked up, and his face blanched with fear.

It was the little Jew, who, having escaped like an eel from Manasseh's care after the Battle of Ohod, and having become thoroughly frightened at the idea of remaining longer in a war-ridden district, had disappeared like magic from the plains of Arabia, and had become once more the insignificant Jewish peddler in the more secure provinces to the north.

"Do not be frightened," laughed Manasseh. "We no longer take prisoners of war; yet, for the sake of old acquaintance, I claim you to partake of our feast."

The little man was half dragged to the table and given a place by Nathan, who spoke kindly to him. Yet he did not feel at ease. The stolen cup seemed to point an accusing finger at him; and he ate little, and talked less.

Presently he caught a glimpse of Yusuf. The sight of the man whom he had so nearly delivered to death was too much for him. His little eyes darted about as if suspicious of some design upon his freedom. He could not understand the magnanimity of these people, and, deeming discretion the better part of valor, he sprang from the table, shouldered his pack, and was off, to be seen no more.

CHAPTER XXXIII.

THE FAREWELL.

"Sondry folk, by aventure y-falle in felaweschipe."
—Chaucer.

And now, our tale draws to a close, and time permits but a parting glance at those who have been so long a goodly company of friends.

Amzi has, in his descent to old age, developed a wonderful activity of mind and body. He has become one of the most influential members of the little town in which he has taken up his abode. Realizing as never before the duty which man owes to man, and fully awakened at last to the fact that our talents are given us to be exercised fully, he no longer dreams away time in the Arab Kaif; but, from morning to night, his plump figure and good-natured old face are seen, up and down, in the mart, in the council-chamber, in the church, wherever he can lend a helping hand. He has even assumed the role of schoolmaster, and upon the earthen floor of an unused hall he gathers day by day a troop of little ones, over whom he bends patiently as they cling to his gown for sympathy in their small trials, or as they trace upon their wax tablets, with little, uncertain hands and in almost illegible characters, the words of a copy, or text.

"Aye," he says, "who knows what these little ones may some day become? They are as impressionable as the wax upon which they write. Heaven grant that the impression made upon them may be mighty for good!"

Kedar has married a Bedouin maid, and is happy in his free life in the old land. Naught but the desert could satisfy him; he would stagnate in the calm life which those in the Jordan valley are finding so pleasant.

As yet he and Manasseh have not been molested in their work by the Moslems; and in their remote mountain recesses they are persistently fighting against heathendom, and are leading many to live better and nobler lives.

And Yusuf? He is in his homeland again. Once more he stands upon the highest point of the Guebre temple. The priests have not refused him admittance, for no one has recognized in this harmless old man the once Guebre Yusuf.

Ah, it is heathen Persia still! The fires flicker upon the altar, and the idolatrous chants arise on the air. Yusuf covers his face with his mantle and weeps. He has but a few years of strength before him, but he will spend them in trying to bring the Gospel of love to these poor, blind people.

He grieves for his benighted country; but when the moon slowly rises, shedding her soft rays over the old scene, the mountains, the valleys below, all calm, peaceful, radiant, he is comforted. He thinks of Him who "created the lesser orb to rule the night," and a great joy fills his heart that he has been led to a recognition of Him, and that he has been enabled to lead others to Him.

His face glows with serene happiness and hope. He raises his eyes to the calm, deep heavens, and says:

"O Father, I thank thee that 'mine eyes have seen the King, the Lord of hosts,' and his dear Son! I thank thee that thou hast led me to see Truth! O God, thou hast taught me from my youth, and hitherto have I declared thy wondrous works! Now also when I am old and gray-headed, O God, forsake me not until I have showed thy strength unto this generation, and thy power to every one that is to come! And now, Father, 'what wait I for? My hope is in thee,' the great God, the ever-loving Father, now and for evermore. Amen and amen."

And there will we leave him.

> *"May he live*
> *Longer than I have time to tell his years!*
> *Ever beloved and loving, may his rule be!*
> *And when old Time shall lead him to his end,*
> *Goodness and he fill up one monument!"*
>
> —Shakespeare.

THE END

Printed in the United States
103065LV00006B/408/A

9 781557 425263